M000102622

All rights are reserved & retained
by Michael and Khara Campbell ©2019

This is a work of fiction from the authors and are not meant to depict, portray, or represent any particular person.

Names, characters, places, and incidents are either the product of the author's imagination or are used fictitiously, and any resemblances to an actual person living or dead are entirely coincidental.

Foreword

Michael Campbell writes with passion and compassion about the very things most of us are faced with today. Michael's words will draw you in and take you on a journey to find your true identity in Christ, despite all of the chaos of society. Michael writes of some of the most entangled struggles of life – you will emerge not only as a fighter, but as a person of faith. You will be all the better in your journey of life when you read this valuable story.

- *David G. Huffman*
  Senior Pastor
  South Potomac Church
  White Plains, Maryland

Gratitude

Special thanks to my wife Khara Campbell for making this book a reality. Thank you to my son Judah, and a few other beta readers: Lisa Monroe, Michelle Monroe, Deb Oelschlage, Cindy Schwimmer, Michael Jones, Davidetta Dave Mal, Nancy Eichelberger, Myra Hannah, Dinah Canton-Johnson, Jerry Candore and Mellisa Williams.

Please forgive me if I missed someone. Your feedback for this book was beneficial in making this happen.

Journey to Faith

Michael Campbell

With Khara Campbell

Introduction

"For I know the thoughts that I think toward you, saith the LORD, thoughts of peace, and not of evil, to give you an expected end." (Jeremiah 29:11)

I was watching television and saw a news flash from CNN. *Breaking News: At least 20 people dead, 26 wounded in El Paso, Texas, in a Walmart shooting ... Breaking News: El Paso shooter identified as a 21-year-old Texas man ... Breaking News: Patrick Crusius is from Allen, Texas, and is believed to be a white supremacist ... Breaking News: President calls the shooting in Texas an act of cowardness.*

I went to bed early that night. When I woke up in the wee hours of the morning, I received an alert on my phone about a shooting. I assumed it might have been an update on the shooting in Texas. *Breaking News: Nine people dead and at least 26 injured in shooting in Dayton, Ohio, approximately 13 hours after the shooting in Texas ... Breaking News: Ohio gunman's sister is among the nine people killed by Connor Betts.*

How does faith make sense in such heartbreaking tragedies? How does faith filter the pain, the hurt, the anguish, the uncertainty these tragedies bring? Why does God allow suffering? Why does God allow pain? Can we trust God when life doesn't make sense?

Recently I received a friend request on Facebook from someone I have not seen in about thirty years. They wanted to reconnect, so I had the option to accept or reject the friend request. I believe God inspired me to write this book, *Journey to Faith,* as a tool for Him to extend His friend request to us. He wants us to *know* Him, not know *of* Him. God doesn't want you to know of Him through your praying grandmother, mother/father, or even pastor. He wants you to know Him *personally*. The way you do a friend. So, the question is, will you accept this friend request from the Almighty?

God wants you to lay aside any hurt, any pain, any anger you feel toward Him. Give Him a new chance to build a relationship with you. He wants you to lay aside any prejudice you have toward Him. The word prejudice means to judge something without having truth or evidence about a person or thing.

For some of us, most of the information we have about God is secondhand information. It is like going to court and being convicted of a crime without due process, without the facts and truth. It would be unconstitutional to be convicted without the judge and jury knowing the facts. If this is true for us not to be judged without proper information, could it be that we have judged God without the proper information?

The beautiful thing about a friend request is that you can always unfriend a person. Well, you can unfriend God if what you learn about Him isn't what you like. But at least accept the invitation to know the Creator of the heavens and earth. What do you have to lose?

Recently, I received a letter in the mail; it was from a credit card company letting me know, *Mr. Campbell, you have been pre-approved to receive this visa credit card. All you need to do is accept.* Well, guess what? God wants us to know we have been pre-approved to become His friend. Your past doesn't matter and nor does your mistakes, hurts, or regrets, nothing matters! All you have to do is say, "Yes, I will accept His friend request."

I'm a member of a local tennis club in Alexandria, Virginia. My tennis instructor, Mark, showed me a picture of himself and a person I didn't immediately recognize. This person looked to be in his mid-sixties, gray hair, and he was wearing glasses. Mark asked, "Do you recognize him?"

I replied, "No, should I?"

"Aww, man, you don't know who Bill Gates is?"

I looked at the picture again closely and recognized Bill Gates. Mark displayed a giddy-cheesy grin. I figure I'd have a giddy-cheesy look, too, if I had met Bill Gates. Know what's amazing? Most of us know God like Mark knew Bill Gates; yet, it's not an intimate relationship. It's a relationship without any substance or meaning.

God desires to have a close intimate friendship with you. He wants you to know Him as well as He knows you. I'm asking you to accept the pre-approved invitation He has extended right now and to know what He's offering is priceless—to become a son or daughter of the Almighty God!

Let us take this *Journey to Faith*, a fictional story with biblical truths of faith in God, together. Let us lay aside any prejudice, hurt, or anger, and get to know Jehovah for ourselves.

-   *Michael Campbell*

Synopsis

Marcia Jackson, a forty-nine-year-old widow, has been struggling with her faith for many years. The unexpected death of her devoted husband thirteen years ago left her alone to raise three children growing up in Southern Maryland.

She is desperately praying to God for answers on where her life is going and what's her purpose. Marcia's journey to faith leads her on a path to meeting forty-nine-year-old Thomas Banks, and several other people, who unknowingly becomes connected through a series of events. They all begin asking God, why? In time, they will all receive their answers. But will their answers be what they all expected?

Journey to Faith is a fictional story with topical biblical truths.

Chapter 1

"And call upon me in the day of trouble: I will deliver thee, and thou shalt glorify me." (Psalm 50:15)

Why does God allow us to wait? Why is He silent? Why does He sometimes answer us in ways we don't expect?

Being a mom was tough; being a single mom was even tougher. At least, that's what it felt like to Marcia Jackson. She was exhausted from working as an information technology specialist at a Charles County, Maryland, middle school, and staying behind two hours to resolve some technical issues with the internet server. She envied the teachers that got the summers off. But Marcia was thankful for the overtime pay she would receive in a few days. She just wanted to get home and get in bed. Then Marcia remembered groceries were needed if she and her children were to eat tonight, tomorrow morning, and the day after that until payday.

After parking her old model sedan, she made a mental note of the items needed to purchase before heading into the store. Marcia looked the way she felt – tired. Her polished ponytail that morning was now disheveled, and her dark pants and white blouse were wrinkled.

While walking down the grocery aisle, Marcia was doing a lot of praying. It seemed she prayed more in the supermarket than anywhere else. *Jesus, please, allow my card to go through!* And every time, without exception, it worked. Marcia was a single mother of three children. Her husband died suddenly from a seizure while on vacation in Fort Lauderdale, Florida, thirteen years ago.

Marcia's life was shattered. She felt lost without purpose and direction. For years, Marcia fought spiritual doubt by asking God, "Why did You allow this to happen?"

The grocery store was packed, and after fifteen minutes of waiting, Marcia was the next person in line. The cashier rung up her groceries, which came to $45.67 after the store discount. Marcia remembered she had about $60 in her account from the last time she checked a few hours ago. Inwardly, she was praying, *Please, don't let it get decline.*

"Debit, credit, or cash?" the cashier asked.

Marcia replied with hesitation and a squeaky voice, "Debit, please." She swiped her card then put in the PIN. Waiting nervously for the card to successfully process, she looked at the cashier, then noticed the people standing behind were becoming impatient. It seemed the card didn't work according to the message on the machine. *Maybe the chip isn't working*. Marcia pulled out the card and wiped it along the sleeve of her shirt then re-inserted it while silently praying.

After a few excruciatingly long seconds, the cashier announced, "Your card is declined." Everyone in the line was upset at the thought of a manager having to be called to prolong the wait.

Suddenly, it seemed from nowhere; a man said, "I will pay." Marcia had mixed emotions; she was happy God had answered her prayer but didn't like the way used to do so. *Why is this white man helping me, a black woman?* But she graciously accepted the gentleman's offer.

Marcia waited outside to thank the man who had helped her. "What is your name?" she asked, approaching the white male as he exited the grocery store. He was much taller than her five feet, six inches height. Marcia assumed he had to be a couple inches over six feet. He had the greenest eyes she'd ever seen and she knew she would never forget them. Unlike her looking and feeling a mess, the gentleman in front of her was neatly dressed in khaki pants and a blue polo shirt.

"Thomas," he replied.

"Why did you do that?" she asked, desperate to know.

Thomas looked at her kindly, "It was the right thing to do. Now just pass on the generosity."

As Marcia drove home from the store, she was struggling and torn that God would answer her prayer the way He did. She continued to play the scene over and over in her head. There was one thing for sure; God had intervened in her life, and God was concerned about her.

Working as an IT specialist at a public school, she didn't make much of a salary. Right before her husband died, they had barely managed to purchase a house, considering all the debt they had. Her two children, Jada, aged fourteen who had an outgoing personality, James, aged sixteen, who took his role as man of the house seriously, were from her deceased husband.

The twenty-year-old, Lisa, who was like a second mother to her siblings, was from a previous relationship. The government benefits received, for her teens after her husband's death, were just enough to cover the mortgage. But Marcia still had other bills. Being a single parent of three children was overwhelming and expensive. It seemed as if she was always managing a crisis.

At forty-nine years old, Marcia still struggled with self-doubt. She constantly asked, "God, who am I? Why am I here? What can I do? And where am I going?" Desperately praying as she drove home, her thoughts were racing too much to get clarity. Marcia needed a clear mind, so she turned on the radio. A song by Lauren Daigle titled "You Say" was playing.

The words to the song brought tears of joy and hope to Marcia's eyes. She felt the presence of God in a way she'd never felt it before. Like in the grocery store, she knew beyond a shadow of a doubt God had answered her prayer. *Jesus, did You really just answer my prayer through a song lyric?*

When Marcia finally arrived home, she logged onto YouTube and found the song. She sat and listened to it twenty times that night.

Chapter 2

"The steps of a good man are ordered by the LORD: and he delighteth in his way." (Psalms 37:23)

Have you ever considered that God has ordained your life for such a time as this? That you were born the year you were supposed to be born and not 100 years earlier or later? You are not an accident.

Thomas Banks had a rough day, making him tired and distracted. It didn't help that he was driving in a rainstorm. The windshield wipers were on their fastest speed and still didn't make the road ahead visible. He decided to take a shortcut home.

Unfortunately, this route had no streetlights and many twists and turns. Thomas heard his phone ringing, but it fell between the seat when he attempted to answer it. When he reached down to pick it up, he noticed a car stopped partially on the side of the road. With little time to react, he almost sideswiped the car but managed to come to a complete stop safely. He pulled over to the side of the road, got out to assist, and noticed a woman by herself in the car, at least from what he could make out in the rain.

He approached the old model red sedan and knocked on the window and asked, "Do you need some assistance?" With the rain pouring down on him, Thomas needed a moment to compose himself.

"Thomas?" she asked, looking up at him through the crack in the partially rolled down window.

Recognizing the lady's voice, Thomas turned to get a better look at her. However, this was quite difficult as the cold rain pelted down on his face. As Thomas gazed down on this woman, his mouth dropped in pure disbelief. *Is this the lady from the grocery store?*

"I'm Marcia, the woman from the grocery store yesterday. You paid for my groceries." Marcia could never forget his forest green eyes.

"Yes, I remember. Interesting how we're meeting again."

She smiled. "Yes, and again, you're at my rescue."

Thomas was soaked and desperately wanted to get home. "I'll have to somehow push your car more to the side of the road. With the heavy rain and lack of visibility, it's not safe for you to be sitting here like this. It can cause an accident! I almost slammed into you."

"Thank you! I appreciate your help. The tow truck is on its way."

After Thomas safely pushed the car to the side of the road, he noticed headlights from a car speeding toward them. When it stopped, two men wearing dark hoodies jumped out of the vehicle. Thomas had a bad feeling about the two men as they approached them. One wasted no time pulling out a handgun. "Give us the keys to your car, wallet, and cell phones."

Marcia screamed, "Please, please! Don't hurt us! I have kids I want to go home to." She silently sent up a prayer to God.

Thomas thought, *This really has been a bad day.*

The rain had slightly let up but was still heavily coming down. The man with the gun lifted his weapon higher toward Thomas, but it slipped out of his grasp. The other man tried to get the weapon but Thomas lunged forward, kicking the gun out of the way while he also pulled out his service revolver and aimed it toward the men. "Charles County police, put your hands up!"

Chapter 3

"And we know that all things work together for good to them that love God, to them who are called according to his purpose." (Romans 8:28)

What are you facing right now that doesn't make any sense? Are you angry with God? Are you disappointed? When we allow the broken pieces of our lives to come together, each piece has its own purpose, whether good or bad. God can use any circumstance and change it for our betterment. Remember, God only wants the best for us, and even during hardship, those times are moments when God is strengthening us and preparing us for greater things.

Think of a caterpillar that forms a cocoon to transform into a butterfly; this is called a metamorphosis – the process of change. This process of transformation is slow and difficult. But the result is a miracle: a butterfly. Right now, some of you may be in a cocoon, but soon you will see that God is working everything out for your good.

Thomas was a forty-nine-year-old divorced father to a twenty-two-year-old son named Karter. He had been employed with the Charles County Police Department for twenty-four years and was almost ready to retire. In all of his years as an officer, he had never experienced a night like he just had. Back at the station, after the attempted robbery and carjacking, he needed to process and fingerprint the two criminals.

God, this has been a tough day. Earlier that day, Thomas was the lead detective on a case of an accidental drowning at a local pool. At the University of Maryland Charles Regional Medical Center, he was with the father of the nine-year-old boy who drowned. Seeing the sorrow and anguish in the father's eyes was heartbreaking.

Thomas had never shown emotion or shed a tear on the job. He tried hard not to so that his emotions didn't interfere with doing his job. Thomas put a wall up to try and protect himself from negative emotions. Working as a police officer, Thomas had seen sad, unsettling, and depressing things. He made a vow years ago to never take work home with him.

Thomas overheard the father calling the child's mother. The call was to let the mother know their son Little John was dead. Thomas overheard the disbelief in the mother's voice. She asked, "John who?"

And the father confirmed, "Our son Little John is dead!"

In all the years of Thomas being a police officer, he had never felt so broken. He was overcome with compassion for these parents and at a loss for words. They had just lost their nine-year-old son, and now he had to ask this father what happened. Thomas felt as if he was further rubbing salt in the fresh wound. Thomas didn't understand why this was getting to him. He'd dealt with death cases many times before, and none have carried the sheer gravity of what he witnessed today.

He felt genuine empathy for Little John's father, but things only got worse. Little John's mother rushed to the hospital in a state of hysteria. She barged into the room where Little John was lying, as his soulless body rested on the medical table. Little John's mother cried, hugging her son until his body turned cold, screaming, "My son! My son!"

Thomas shook his head, clearing his thoughts from earlier today. After processing and booking the two men, Thomas noticed Marcia sitting alone on the bench in the reception area of the police station. It had been a couple of hours since the incident, and she still looked traumatized.

He brought her a cup of coffee. "How are you holding up?"

Accepting the foam cup filled with coffee, she gave a faint smile. "I'm glad to be alive." She took a sip of the bitter drink. "Thank you for everything. Paying for my groceries the other day and coming to my rescue tonight."

"You're welcome. Apparently, God knows when you need help, and He sends me to the rescue."

They shared a laugh.

"Is someone picking you up?" Thomas looked at his watch and noticed it was almost ten.

She looked at him sheepishly. "I was hoping I could ask you for a ride home. With my car towed to the mechanic ..."

"Sure, it won't be a problem. I was about to leave. I guess you can add this to your running list of heroic things I do for you," he joked.

She smiled, liking that thought.

Two weeks later:

Thomas attended Little John's funeral that was held at a church in Waldorf, Maryland. It was a sad, surreal, and unfair occasion. Little John had a small, white casket, and looked like he was sleeping peacefully. Thomas was shocked when Little John's father, John Sr., got up to speak. He was a well-spoken man in his mid thirties. Thomas thought there was no way he would be able to do so if he were in the father's shoes.

As John Sr., spoke, he glanced down, paused, and then continued. "The God I serve is a God of comfort. He enables me to stand before you today. With hope in Him, I know I will see Little John again. Like any father, like any parent, I would want my son to live a long life; longevity has its place. As David said in Second Samuel 12:23, 'Nothing can bring him back, but one day, I will go to where my son is.' You may not believe this, but everyone who said a kind word of love, support, and encouragement, I remembered. Thank you. You never imagine that you would have to eulogize your son."

The father asked for everyone to pray for Little John's mother, Korrine. "She's a good mother. I would ask all of you to pray for her in a time like this." He prayed that this tragedy could finally bring healing between two families as he and the mother were divorced, and both families were suffering an enormous loss today. "I want to share a story about a jigsaw puzzle Little John and I were putting together. He said, 'Daddy, this puzzle doesn't make sense!'

I said, "This is only a small piece of the puzzle, son.' He was only looking at the small portion we had completed, and there were so many other parts left to be connected." The father looked down as if gathering strength. "Little John's death is a piece of God's puzzle. Nobody has to be in their seventies or eighties to accomplish their purpose in life. I pray one day that I will fully understand the tragic loss of my son better." He wiped tears from his eyes and then quoted a lyric from the song entitled "*By and By*."

"By and by, when the morning comes, all the saints of God are gathering home, and we'll tell the story of how we overcome, and we'll understand it better, by and by."

Chapter 4

"Trust in the LORD with all thine heart, and lean not unto thine own understanding. In all thy ways acknowledge him, and he shall direct thy paths." (Proverbs 3:5-6)

When and why do we use our GPS (Global Positioning System)? The purpose of a GPS is to take us where we want to go. Sometimes a GPS can be frustrating because it will lead you down a road that you don't want to take. But I have learned time and time again to trust what it says because it sees what I can't see. How much more does God see what we don't see? Our job is to trust what He says and do what He says.

Marcia had two daughters; Lisa was twenty and about to go to Spelman College in Atlanta. Jada was fourteen and heading to high school. Marcia was concerned that with the absence of her oldest daughter, there would be a void because they had been a close family, especially since her husband's death thirteen years ago. She didn't want their family bond broken. The notion of Lisa leaving for college had given Marcia a feeling of loneliness and sadness, a feeling she constantly battled.

Marcia's son, James, was sixteen. He received his learner's permit a few months ago and was now ready to take the test for his driver's license. It was scheduled for next month. As Marcia struggled with singlehood, she was finding that her children were starting to become less and less dependent on her. She was trying to find her place in the world again with her children gaining more independence. Marcia was celibate since the death of her husband and hadn't dated often.

Sitting on the couch, catching up on one of her favorite series, Grey's Anatomy, on Netflix, Marcia's cellphone rang from the coffee table in front of her. Pausing the show, she picked up her phone. The sight of Thomas' name on the screen sent a chill up her spine. She unconsciously smiled. She had saved his number that night he brought her home from the police station. That was a couple of weeks ago.

"Hey," Marcia answered, not caring if she sounded too giddy.

Thomas couldn't help his smile either at the sound of her pleasant voice. He quickly reminded himself this wasn't a personal call; he was calling as a police officer. "Hi, Marcia. I'm calling to tell you a court date has been scheduled for three weeks from today; Tuesday at ten."

"Oh, sure. I should be able to make it; that's enough time to let my supervisor know."

"Good. It would help a lot having you there, too." He meant for the case but also because he wanted to see her again. "How have you been?"

"A little more anxious, especially driving at night. But I've been reciting second Timothy 1:7."

"For God hath not given us the spirit of fear, but of power, and love, and a sound mind." He quoted the Scripture. "Has it been helping?"

"It has." She was impressed he knew that Scripture. "So, not only are you a superhero, you're a man of faith?"

Thomas smiled while replying. "That I am."

They were quiet for a moment, lost in their own thoughts. "How are your kids? I remember you mentioned your daughter Lisa is getting ready to leave for college."

Marcia was shocked that he remembered such details. The ride from the police station to her home was only twenty minutes, and they both talked about their kids. "They're all doing well, enjoying their last few weeks of summer break. James will be taking the test for his driver's license soon. Jada is enjoying cheer camp, and Lisa is enjoying her paid internship at Charles County Government. I'm the one miserable because I'm not ready for her to leave, although she's just going off to college now at twenty." Lisa had completed her associate degree at the College of Southern Maryland and would be heading to Spelman College in Atlanta in a few short weeks to finish up her bachelor's.

"I was the same way when my son left for Stanford University in California. It will get easier as time passes."

"I hope so. How is Karter? How does he like being home for the summer?"

"He's good but hardly ever home. He got an internship for the summer with the Department of State. When he's not working, he's catching up with friends leaving not much time to hang out with his old pops." He chuckled.

"Kids!" Marcia laughed. "And you're not old. We're the same age, so I can't have you thinking you're old, which means you think I'm old."

Thomas imagined her beautiful mocha-colored skin and how youthful she looked despite her forty-nine years. "Yeah, you're not old."

Marcia blushed from hearing his flirtatious tone.

"Would you like to go out for breakfast the morning before court?" He asked at the spur of the moment, hoping he wasn't overstepping bounds.

"Yes!" Marcia practically shouted. She couldn't contain her excitement at a possible date with Thomas. She was of practice with dating; she hadn't realized that perhaps she should play it cool. Marcia hadn't been interested in a man since her husband. And she'd never found herself attracted to a white man before but was drawn to Thomas' forest green eyes and salt and pepper hair.

Thomas was still at work and needed to go. "Good. We'll plan something closer to the date. It was nice talking to you."

"You, too. Enjoy the rest of your day and stay safe."

"You do the same, Marcia."

Chapter 5

"Delight thyself also in the LORD: and he shall give thee the desires of thine heart." (Psalms 37)

What does desire mean? Desire is not so much what we want, but desire has to be sanctioned. Our desire has to be in harmony with God's desire, as well. As we spend more time with God, our desire and His desire become inseparable. It's the same way that coffee changes the state of water.

Marcia was getting prepared to meet Thomas at IHOP. She was nervous but also excited. While standing in the bathroom applying makeup, she stared at herself. *Is this really a date, or is he just being nice in suggesting breakfast before going to court?* As she sprayed her favorite perfume and finished brushing her hair, she whispered, "Girl, you look good today!"

James had gotten up early that morning. He was preparing to study for his driving test. When Marcia walked into the living room, James noticed her and said, "Mom, you look great!"

"Don't I always look great?" she replied with a playful smile.

"Of course, mom, but you look extra good today!"

"Well, at least one man thinks so. Hopefully, Thomas feels the same way." Marcia had already informed her kids she needed to go to court for the attempted carjacking that happened a while back.

"Do I need to chaperone?" he asked, smirking. James was happy to see his mom going out on a date. This was probably his first time seeing her do so.

"Boy, quit playing! I'm grown!" They laughed. She walked over and kissed him on the forehead before leaving the house.

After getting into the car, Marcia turned on the radio. The song "You Say" by Lauren Daigle came on. Hearing this song once more in this situation triggered the same emotions she felt when she heard the song the first time that day when Thomas paid for her groceries. It was as if God was confirming that He was with her, and Marcia was moving in the right direction.

As she pulled up to the IHOP, Marcia said a quick prayer. "Not my will, but Your will be done today, Lord." She checked herself again in the rear-view mirror then exited the car.

Thomas texted her while she was driving that he was already seated. He noticed her approaching the table. He stood to greet her in awe again of her beauty and even more so as this was his first time seeing her dressed up. The first time he met her at the grocery store her clothes were unmemorable and the second time, the night of the incident, she was dressed casually in jeans and a plain t-shirt. Today, she sported a black skirt suit with a white blouse and black heels. Marcia looked ladylike and attractive.

He surprised Marcia by enveloping her in a hug.

The fresh woodsy scent of his cologne awakened something dormant inside of her; she knew his scent would stay in her thoughts all day.

"You look gorgeous." He reluctantly pulled away from the embrace.

She smiled up at him; her heart was beating rapidly. The chemistry between them was undeniable.

"Thank you. You look nice in a suit. Is this court day attire?" He had on a gray suit minus a tie.

"Thanks. Yes, it is." He pulled out a chair for her.

After placing their orders, he said, "I invited you to breakfast so I can go over what will happen in court today."

Marcia's excitement about their meeting deflated. *This really was a date. Am I that out of practice with men? He's a cop. Of course, he just wants to reassure me about the case. He's doing his job. I had to make it seem like something more, and he's white; maybe he isn't attracted to black women.*

Thomas went on to tell her what should happen when they arrived at the courthouse.

***

The two African American defendants confessed to the attempted armed robbery and carjacking and took a plea deal. The state's attorney asked for a sentence between eight to five years in state prison.

Judge Richard Claire, a short white man with a receding hairline, asked Marcia if there was anything she wanted to say before he passed down the sentence.

She nervously stood, looked at Thomas sitting beside her, giving her an encouraging smile. "No," she answered, wringing her hands, but suddenly changed her mind. "On second thought, I do have something I want to say." Her eyes moved from the judge to the two defendants. With a potent tone of anger, she asked, "Why would you try to hurt somebody? What were you guys thinking when you did this?"

One of the defendants was named Bobby, and he was nineteen years old. He was the aggressor of the two and felt no remorse for what he did. Paul, the other defendant, was eighteen years old, and his conscious was torn over what he did.

Paul said in a devastated tone, "Ma'am, I'm so sorry," his voice cracked. "Please, forgive me! I'm so sorry."

Paul's mother died four years ago, and he was living with his aunt. He never knew his father. And even though Bobby was only a year older than him, he was the brother and friend Paul needed – at least Paul thought he needed. Bobby defended him against the bullies when they were in school, and their friendship blossomed from there. Bobby was obviously a bad influence. But not having a father and mother figure in his life, Paul feeds off of their negative friendship. *At least someone was looking out for me.*

With just that simple, heartfelt apology, Marcia was filled with compassion and forgiveness. She forgot the anger she had moments ago. She thought her son James was only a few years younger than both of these young men. "Son, I forgive you. But what you did was wrong. But I serve a God of second chances."

Paul couldn't believe she had forgiven him so quickly. He began sobbing like never before. He thought about his dead mother and how disappointed she would've been of him. But Marcia's forgiveness would help heal his heart. He couldn't remember the last time somebody had called him son. It was as if God had allowed their two paths to meet.

Judge Claire brought the attention back to himself and announced, "You two young men have made a bad mistake. But your life isn't over. One of you has shown remorse. Because this is your first offense, I sentence you to six years in the state penitentiary." He slammed his gavel, "This court is adjourned!"

The sheriff led Paul and Bobby out of the courtroom. Paul looked back at Marcia with a smile of hope and gleam in his eyes. Despite being sentenced to six years in prison, Paul had a sense of hope for the first time, but there was still a long road ahead for him. Right then and there, Marcia promised she would write to Paul while he was incarcerated.

Thomas held the door open for Marcia to leave the courtroom. Since the second time he saw her, he'd been fighting his attraction to her. He really did ask her out to breakfast for more than just giving her a heads up about court today. He had an intense need to spend more time with her. Since Marcia gave him her cellphone number the night of the attempted robbery, he had to force himself not to call her every day. He was trying hard to keep their interactions professional; things had to stay professional and platonic.

After surviving a bitter divorce eight years ago, Thomas was man enough to admit he had some insecurities toward diving into a relationship. His whole divorce experience was traumatic, and he was still dealing with the side effects.

Silently, they walked to her car. He indulgently let his eyes sweep over her beautiful facial features. "It was really nice seeing you today, despite the reason."

"It was nice seeing you, too, Thomas." Believing he wasn't attracted to her like she was to him, Marcia was anxious to leave before saying something stupid like let's go out to dinner. She wasn't in the mood for being rejected. She pulled her key out of her purse to unlock the car door. It was weird; Marcia felt like he was breaking up with her when they weren't even dating. This was her third time seeing this man, and she already missed him, and he was standing before her, especially knowing this would probably be the last time they saw each other. *Maybe I need to sign up for Christian Mingle?*

"Take care of yourself."

Chapter 6

"For now, we see through a glass, darkly; but then face to face: now I know in part; but then shall I know even as also I am known." (1 Corinthians 13:12)

I was backing out of a parking space, and I couldn't see anything behind me. I asked someone if they could watch while I backed up. As they were guiding me out, I suddenly got a revelation of what journey to faith means. We don't have to see what is behind or what is in front of us. Having faith in God means looking to Him for direction and not at the things around us.

It had been three weeks since Marcia saw Thomas. She was starting to feel sorry for herself. Although she wasn't questioning God, she had no peace; she felt helpless about her future and sad about the past. Marcia was struggling to make sense of the present.

She missed Thomas. From the first moment Marcia met him, she felt God had ordained him to come into her life. Thomas rescued her not once, but twice. That couldn't be just a coincidence. No way could she believe it was just happenstance! *If that's so, why hasn't he called me? I really thought he was interested in me, like I am interested in him.*

Marcia huffed a breath; her body was sore from working out two hours at the gym. She needed a way to relieve stress and pushing her body to the limit on the treadmill and kickboxing, was it. Not only was she heartbroken from things not going anywhere with Thomas, her daughter Lisa was leaving for college soon, and James was getting his driver's license. Marcia retrieved her gym bag from the backseat of the car. She had to get to bed early to take James to take his driver's test in the morning.

She walked into her house through the garage. In the kitchen, she noticed the dishes weren't washed. Marcia decided to load the dishwasher. While she was tiding up, something on the small television mounted on the wall caught her attention. *Breaking News: White supremacist group has declared war on immigrants, Blacks, and non-whites. Unlike before, the white supremacist group said they would make America great again.*

Marcia stood stunned from hearing the breaking news. A clip from a white supremacist speaking continued. "Mr. President, we hear you, and we will not be replaced." Marcia shook her head in disbelief. She felt what her grandmother felt in the 50s and 60s. *How could this be happening in America right now?* For the first time in her life, Marcia didn't feel safe in her own country.

Dan Linton, the host of the news show, *What's Happening in America*, looked sternly and seriously into the television screen. It was as if he was reporting on the end of the world as we knew it. "Ladies and gentlemen, did you hear what was just said?" Dan paused in disbelief as if even he didn't believe what he was saying. "Let me try to make this easy for you to digest. There has been a declaration of war on all of those who are non-white.

This is something I would never, ever imagine I would see, talk about, or report. As you know, I have been reporting the news for years, and nothing has come close to this current situation. I wonder how our president, Calvin Johnson, will try to escape the urgent questions of the American people this time? How is he going to wiggle his way out of this? How will he explain why this is happening? What will he do? The terrorists are repeating and using the words Johnson himself has claimed!"

With an intense tone and anger, Dan Linton pointed his finger at the screen, shouting, "I will blame you for every drop of blood spilled over the phrase *Make America great again*, Mr. Johnson! I will blame you for every innocent person slain in the name of racial discrimination! You have fueled the rhetoric of this hatred, this mindset, and this ideology to those foolish enough to act upon it! How is this normal?

Who would have expected that the leader of the free world would be admired by bigots, people who hate and ridicule other races, and people who despise another person for where they were born? How could this be?"

Marcia's eyes were glued to the screen in pure shock, fear, and disbelief. She was trying to process what she was hearing but continuously drew blanks. She tried to think, but the fear manifested around her like a black, booming thunderstorm. She continued listening.

"Ladies and gentlemen, please, excuse my previous interjections. I didn't mean to let my emotions get the best of me. I have a special guest, the Reverend Al Sharpton." Reverend Sharpton was in the studio with Linton. The cameras turned to him.

"Reverend Sharpton, what are your thoughts on this war that has been declared on non-whites due to our president?"

"Well, Dan, it is as if I had gotten into a time capsule and transported back into 1965. Words cannot express how sad it is that a time such as 1965, where there seemed to be limitless hatred, vicious dogs being turned on people, women being raped, and men being murdered, could be compared to modern-day. And certainly, our president can't control what people do, but he undeniably has inflamed a situation that would reunite the hatred that's been dormant in our society for so long."

Dan Linton attentively took note of Sharpton's words, then replied, "Mr. Sharpton, I pray this was a hoax, and I pray nothing becomes of this. But where there is smoke, there is generally fire."

"I pray, too, Dan. The thing about it is, we are at the mercy of these ignorant fools! We don't have enough police to monitor every shopping center, every McDonald's, and every movie theatre! We shouldn't be afraid of dying when we go to these places simply because we do fit the description of being non-white!

We don't and never will have the manpower to do that! We need our president to be the president of every American, no matter if they are black, white, orange, or yellow. He should not be selective in who he wants to lead.

Marcia turned off the television in disbelief, took a deep breath in an attempt to calm her nerves. *Jesus, please, take the wheel. This is crazy!*

After quickly finishing up cleaning the kitchen, Marcia made her way to the bathroom to wash up before bed. She grabbed her toothbrush from the holder. *Lord, this is crazy! A war on non-whites? I can't believe this!* As she applied her toothpaste and started brushing, she paused and said, "Everything will be okay. Jesus, You are bigger than the problems we face."

Chapter 7

"Yea, though I walk through the valley of the shadow of death, I will fear no evil: for thou art with me; thy rod and thy staff they comfort me." (Psalm 23:4)

There's a story about a judge telling a man standing before him in the courtroom that if the man ever stood before the judge again for another DUI, he would sentence him to a night in jail. The man said he understood and promised he wouldn't return. However, sometime later, he did. The judge sentenced him to a night in jail. The man, a war veteran, told the judge he was claustrophobic and afraid he wouldn't be able to handle being in a small jail cell.

But the judge sentenced him to a night in jail anyway. Lo and behold, when the man walked into his cell, the judge was there, too. He came so that the man wouldn't be alone or afraid in his cell. When we walk through the valley of our about deepest despair, the Lord's rod and staff will comfort us.

James sat up in bed at the sound of his alarm clock going off at 7:30 a.m. He groggily reached for his cellphone and turned off the incessant noise. It took him a moment to gather his thoughts. Then he remembered, *I get my driver's license today*. He threw the sheet off and excitedly climbed out of bed. He needed to be at the MVA by 9:30. He did a happy dance as he went to the bathroom to take care of his hygiene before returning to his room to quickly dress.

He knocked on Marcia's bedroom door. "Mom!"

"What is it, James?" she asked from the other side.

"I don't want to be late."

"Oh, now you don't want to be late!" She opened the bedroom door, fully dressed, wearing a warm smile. "My baby isn't a baby anymore." She pulled him into a hug, happy he allowed her to do so. But moments later, he wiggled free.

James started walking toward the front of the house. Marcia trailed behind him. She noticed him heading for the door.

"Don't you want some breakfast first?"

He shook his head. "No, Mom, I will get something to eat after I get my license," he said with confidence.

"Okay, let me check in on your sisters before we leave."

James and Marcia arrived at the MVA at 8:30. He was anxious and excited. Marcia was content with stopping at Wawa to grab a large cup of coffee and a bacon and egg breakfast sandwich. He may not have been hungry, but she needed to eat and fuel up on caffeine.

Before the driving test, the examiner did the usual car inspection before getting into the passenger's seat. James got into the driver's seat, checked his mirrors, and fastened his seat belt. He didn't want to miss any detail that could cause him to fail. When instructed to drive, James took a deep breath then followed the instructor's directions.

Marcia needed to catch up on some work, so she took out her laptop and began working on her latest assignment. After some time passed, she looked at the clock on her laptop and realized it was almost an hour since James went on the driver's test. She hoped he was doing well. A couple of minutes later, she saw James walking toward her with a sad face. His head was slightly bowed, and he seemed humbled. It was all too obvious what had happened.

Standing to greet him, Marcia took a deep breath. "Don't worry; you will pass the test next time."

James shook his head. "No, I won't because I passed this time!"

Marcia playfully shoved him. "Okay, you got me!" She laughed.

***

After completing the necessary paperwork, they left the MVA. James proudly took the driver's seat as a newly licensed driver. His official card would be mailed later.

"Now I'm hungry," he said, starting the engine.

"Let's go to Walmart. I can get some dish detergent and trash bags, and you can get a sandwich from Subway."

Marcia needed to get back to work by noon. Her boss was kind enough to let her take the morning off.

"Okay. Can I drop you off to work and pick you up at three?" He knew he was trying his luck, but it didn't hurt to ask. He wanted the car for the afternoon to maybe go to the movies with friends.

"Nope. You can borrow the car after I get home. And don't forget the safety rules."

"I won't, Mom, promise. My cellphone will be on, *don't disturb while I'm driving*. No riding with a bunch of friends and stay attentive at the wheel." He recited.

"Good. Hopefully, in a few months, I can afford to buy you a used car. I need Lisa to get settled at college first."

James was thrilled. He didn't care what type of car he got as long as it didn't look like a complete dump and drove smoothly. "I have three hundred saved toward a car."

Marcia was shocked and proud. "Really? You've been saving up from your lawn care jobs." He worked part-time with their neighbor, Mr. Lewis, who owned a landscaping business.

"Yes. I know it's been hard for you paying all the bills, and I didn't want you having to worry about money to buy me a car."

Tears welled in her eyes. Marcia reached over and compassionately squeezed James' shoulder. He looked so much like his father. He got his six-three height from him. And at 215 pounds, he could be a linebacker. But he was more into technology than playing sports. Her baby was becoming a man; he sure looked like one. "Thank you." She wiped the tears from her eyes. "And when you get back to school, you may have to keep working part-time to pay for your car insurance because it's going to be high! I was not expecting the quote I received."

"No problem, Mom."

The radio host caught her attention, and Marcia reached over to turn up the volume for the radio. "The Department of Justice is investigating President Johnson on campaign money he allegedly received from North Korea under the guise of a business deal ..."

"What does that mean, Mom?" James asked.

Marcia turned down the radio. "It means the president allegedly made a deal or is working with the enemy, but either way, we must pray for the president – whether we believe in his policies or not."

James nodded.

Marcia's cellphone rang just as James pulled up to Walmart and parked next to a red truck. James noticed a white man in his mid-twenties as he got out of the truck. In the ninety-plus degree weather, James found it strange that the man was wearing a black hooded jacket.

James tapped Marcia's shoulder to get her attention. She was on the phone with her co-worker,

Patrice. "Mom, why does this guy have a jacket on in the middle of summer?"

Still talking to her co-worker, Marcia looked out the window, noticing the man walking toward the entrance of Walmart. She shrugged her shoulder at James, meaning she didn't know.

"Hold on a sec," she said. Marcia muted the phone. "James, get the dish detergent and trash bags, then get a sandwich from Subway. I need to finish my conversation with my co-worker." She reached into her wallet and gave him her debit card.

As James walked into Walmart, Marcia thought about the man with the hooded jacket. With all the crazy stuff she'd seen on the news, she got a bad feeling about it. She shook her head. *You worry too much.*

In the aisle for the dish detergent, James noticed the suspicious young man from the parking lot again. The man looked nervous, which had red flags blaring in James' head. James calmly walked over to another aisle, then peeked over to watch the man. He saw the man pull a pistol from his jacket, lifting it slowly toward a Hispanic worker.

James first thought was to run out of the store. He had enough time to do so. But another thought came to mind. He visualized how many people could be hurt if this man opened fire. James took a deep breath, then decided he would intervene.

James walked down the opposite side of the aisle, hoping to disarm the nervous-looking man. When he got within about two feet of the man, James jumped on him.

The gunman yelled. "Get off me! What are you doing?"

They wrestled. Some of the people thought they were fighting until they noticed there was a gun present. It became a chaotic scene. James was fighting for dear life.

One of the workers screamed, "Call security! And the police!"

In all the chaos, the gun slipped out of the suspect's hand. The impact of the small firearm hitting the floor disrupted the firing mechanism. Suddenly, a single loud echoing shot was fired. The blood of James then flowed on the white tiled floor.

There were screams and people running away from the gunfire.

One of the workers yelled. "Someone call an ambulance, now!"

An announcement was heard on the store speakers: "This is NOT a drill. Please calmly find the nearest exit and leave! I repeat, please leave the store calmly. This is NOT a drill."

There was a stampede of people exiting the store. People were frantically asking for details on what happened. Police quickly arrived at the scene.

Marcia was wondering what was going on. As the store evacuated and the massive crowd grew, she knew something was wrong. Dread settled in her bones. Frantically, she got out of the car and ran toward the entrance of Walmart, fighting through the chaotic crowd surrounding the scene. She tried desperately to get in, but the police did not allow her to proceed. Marcia's heart was beating erratically against her chest. She would have called James, but he'd left his cellphone in the car. Looking around, she didn't see him in the sea of people.

The ambulance pulled up. Paramedics entered the store, pushing a stretcher. Marcia didn't know what happened, but she knew it was tragic.

Thomas was one of the first lead detectives to respond to the emergency call. Right away, he noticed Marcia at the front entranceway. He quickly walked over to her. He would ask himself later how he was able to notice her in the crowd. "Marcia, hey. It's not good to be here right now."

"I can't leave. James is inside. I don't know what's going on!" She had a pained look on her face and worry in her eyes.

"All right. I'll go in and see if I can find James." He gave her a reassuring smile. "Stay over here." He took her hand and walked her over to where the outdoor vending machines were. "I'll be back as soon as I find him. I remember the picture you showed me of your kids."

She nodded with a weak smile, anxiously wringing her hands.

Marcia knew Thomas always came to her rescue, so she had confidence that everything would be okay. It took Thomas about eight minutes to come back outside. Marcia saw the look on his face. Instantly, she felt it was something awful.

Thomas approached her and placed his hand on her shoulder in hopes of giving her some comfort.

"James has been shot. He is still alive, but he has lost a large amount of blood."

When she heard this, she tried to run to the scene to see James. She yelled, "James, my son! Not my baby. Please, I need to see him!"

Thomas held her back, pulling her into his arms. "Marcia, I'll take you to the hospital. They are putting him in the ambulance and working on him." Thomas almost had to carry her to his car. She was hysterical as the paramedics loaded James into the ambulance and transported him to the hospital.

James went into cardiac arrest. His heart stopped, but the paramedics were able to revive him.

Chapter 8

"It is of the LORD's mercies that we are not consumed because His compassions fail not. They are new every morning: great is thy faithfulness." (Lamentations 3:22-23)

When I was about eighteen years old, I was in a season of great sadness and darkness. I was at a low point in my life. I was emotionally broken and discouraged. It was over a combination of many things. My father was out of town, but he knew what I was going through, and he sent me a postcard. On the postcard was a poem called "Footprints in the Sand." The words of this poem made me feel the author wrote it specifically for me. It was the peace and breakthrough I needed.

It seemed only a couple seconds passed before Thomas was pulling up to the hospital, the same hospital he watched Little John's parents cry over their dead son. He didn't like the déjà vu feeling he was getting. The red and blue lights and blaring siren on his patrol car helped tremendously. Marcia barely waited for him to park at the emergency entrance before she bolted out of the car.

"Slow down!" Thomas called after her.

"No, you hurry up! I need to see my son!" The automatic doors weren't opening fast enough and tested her minuscule patience. She ran to the reception desk, asking frantically about her son.

The nurse behind the desk looked up at Marcia from typing something on the computer. "May I help you?"

"My son James was just brought in by ambulance. He was shot." Marcia almost choked on the last word.

The nurse had just entered information on a patient by that name moments ago. "Is it James Jackson?"

"Yes, yes! That's him. I'm his mother. Is he okay?" Tears soaked Marcia's face. She was trying hard not to lose her mind.

"He's in surgery right now, that's all I know. But I can look up which doctor and nurse are attending to him." The nurse started typing on her keyboard but glanced up again when she noticed Thomas. "Detective Thomas, how are you doing?"

"I'm okay. But we need your assistance with information on James Jackson," Thomas replied.

The nurse smiled and nodded. She gave the name of the staff attending to James.

Thomas pulled Marcia away from the reception desk. "I have to go speak with the head nurse. I need you to be calm and wait here for me. I will come back right away with any information I gather." Thomas placed his hand on Marcia's shoulder and looked at her with true compassion. He lifted his hand and wiped some of the tears from her eyes with his thumb.

"Thank you, Thomas." She helplessly watched him walk away as he disappeared behind doors meant only for staff and apparently, detectives.

I need to calm down, or I'm going to pass out. God, please, deliver James from this tragedy. You're in the operating room with him. You're the doctors' and nurses' hands. You're the medicine. You're the healing my son needs. Thank you, Father! She found a vacant seat and sat down. Marcia needed to have faith and not panic and fear the worse.

She thought of her daughters Lisa and Jada and realized she'd left her cellphone in the car still parked at Walmart. She needed to call Lisa and let her know what happened. Marcia went to find a payphone as if they were still around these days.

Thomas waited outside the operating room. One of the nurses shouted, "Doctor! We have the x-rays!" Someone else said James had lost dangerous amounts of blood and needed a blood transfusion.

When one of the nurses came out of the operating room, Thomas asked him, "Is he going to be okay?"

The nurse looked at the badge Thomas had hanging around his neck and then answered. "It's very early, but luckily, the bullet missed the main arteries. He's in critical, but stable condition. It's the best possible scenario right now."

"Thank you, God! He's going to pull through this. He has to," Thomas said after the nurse walked away. He took a deep breath, hoping to regain his composure before walking through the metal doors. He noticed Marcia pacing, sitting down, then standing up again.

Marcia stopped pacing when she saw Thomas walking her way. She stared into his eyes, trying to read him. *Does he have good or bad news?* "Is ... is he okay?"

"He's in stable, but critical condition. They're still working on him, and I'm sure the doctor will be out soon to tell you more."

"Okay. But that's good, right? He's in critical, but stable means good, right?"

"Yes, stable means good." Thomas put the professional aside and gently gathered her into his arms for a hug. "He's going to make it through this, Marcia."

She sobbed against his chest. Marcia hadn't realized how much she needed a hug until that moment. She had to believe God would save her son.

Moments later, she lifted her head from his chest. "I left my cellphone in my car. I need to tell Lisa and Jada about what happened."

Thomas went to pull his cellphone out of his pants pocket, and at the same time, it started to ring. It was Detective Avery, one of the guys on his team, calling. "Let me take this real quick; then you can use my phone to call your daughters."

Marcia nodded, then stepped away to give him some privacy. While he was on the phone, Marcia saw a doctor in scrubs heading toward the reception desk. He spoke with the nurse, who then pointed to

Marcia. She walked briskly over to the desk. "Are you the doctor tending to my son, James Jackson?" Marcia nervously clutched her chest.

"Yes, I'm Dr. Patel. James is in recovery. The bullet missed an artery in his lower abdomen. He, however, lost a lot of blood. We had to do a blood transfusion, which went well. The surgery and all went well; I expect him to make a speedy recovery."

Marcia could have fainted from relief. "Thank you, thank you so much. Dr. Patel. When can I see him?"

"Give us a couple of hours to get him situated; then you can see your son."

"Okay. That's enough time for me to go and get his sisters."

"So good news?" Thomas asked after the doctor left. He was done with his call and overheard most of what was said.

Marcia's smile was wide. She jumped into his arms, and he smoothly caught her. "He's going to be fine." After a moment, they separated. "I have to call the girls, and can you take me to my car?"

"Sure. That was Detective Avery calling. The gunman is in custody. I need to head over to the station for questioning."

"That man could have killed my son or someone else." She was angry. The word of God said to love our enemies, but right now, Marcia hated that man with every fiber of her being. *Jesus, help me!*

"I see a news van just pulled up. We should probably go now unless you want to be interviewed?"

"No. Talking to the media is the last thing on my mind right now," she said.

Chapter 9

"And I will restore to you the years that the locust hath eaten, the cankerworm, and the caterpillar, and the palmerworm, my great army which I sent among you." (Joel 2:25)

Now is the time to repossess the thing the enemy has stolen from us. The reason why I use the word repossess is because when people buy cars and can't make payments, the owner comes and repossesses what belongs to him. What has the enemy stolen from you? Is it your health? Your marriage? Your ministry? Your dream? Now is the time to take back what the enemy has stolen. When Jesus died and rose again, He has given us the authority to take back what the enemy has stolen.

Thomas took Marcia back to Walmart to get her car. She needed to get home to her daughters, then they all would go back to the hospital. When they pulled up, yellow caution tape surrounded the entrance where various news reporters were broadcasting.

Thomas wanted to stay with Marcia to support her. He also needed to handle this case and headed to the station right after making sure Marcia was secured. The suspect was taken into custody and was questioned for several hours. They ran his fingerprints and found several prior charges of drug possession, petty arson, and other minor charges stemming from the age of fifteen. The suspect's name was Ronny Datcher, a twenty-four-year-old white male who lived in Newburg, Maryland, with his parents.

After being fingerprinted, Datcher was taking to the interrogation room.

"You want anything to drink?" Detective Avery asked.

"I'd like a cup of coffee, please." Datcher looked around at the plain décor of the room. He was anxious; his heart was drumming rapidly in his chest.

"Sure, no problem. Are you hungry as well?" He wanted Datcher relaxed to get the most information out of him. Avery, a black man, was a twenty-two-year veteran of the Charles County Police Department. This was the first time a crime such as this had happened in Charles county, an alleged hate crime.

"No, I'd just like some coffee for now," Datcher replied, rubbing his right arm. James had five inches of height and forty pounds of an advantage to him, which made it easy for James to overpower Datcher, nearly breaking his arm. At least that's what it felt like to Datcher. "My arm hurts! That guy was huge."

"Okay. We'll get you some medical attention. But first, allow us to ask you some questions." Thomas walked into the interrogation room, taking a seat next to Avery at the long stainless-steel desk with Datcher facing them. "Why was there only one bullet in your gun?" Both detectives found that fact was strange.

Datcher blankly looked at them.

"What was your purpose for walking into Walmart with a loaded gun? The surveillance camera shows you pulling out your gun and aiming to shoot. If it wasn't for James, someone might have been shot."

Datcher was nervously rocking in his seat, rubbing his injured arm. When Avery mentioned what he had done, Datcher slouched in his chair and shook his head. "Oh, my God, what did I just do?" His body started rocking violently. "Oh my, God, my life is ruined! I need to talk to my mom and dad. Is that possible?"

"You will talk to your parents, but you need to calm down."

Datcher abruptly stilled as if a switch was flipped.

Avery continued. "I need to ask you a few more questions. Are you a part of any neo-Nazi, or Aryan brotherhood type group?"

"No, sir. I'd been smoking crystal meth all night into this morning, and I just—I wanted to make America great again. This infestation of immigrants tarnishes the true beauty of America. I wanted to become a martyr for my country," Datcher confessed.

"What in the world were you thinking? How can you make America great by hurting people? Hate only produces hate. Are you a racist?" Thomas asked. Being on the police force for over twenty years, Thomas had heard many racial jokes and comments from some white officers, who had made him uncomfortable. He'd been in the hot seat a few times questioning some of the white officers about some of their arrests he believed was racially motivated. As a Christian, Thomas thought that no race was superior.

"No, sir. Some of my best friends are black ..."

Thomas and Avery gave each other knowing looks.

"I just wanted to be famous. I just wanted to make a difference. Can I please talk to my mom and dad? I'm sorry; I wasn't thinking straight."

Thomas sternly replied, "You can talk to your lawyer; your mom and dad can't help you now."

"Please, let me go back to my cell. I don't want to talk anymore."

Thomas and Avery tried to get Datcher to talk more, but he refused. After about ten minutes of dead silence, Detective Avery told one of the guards to take Ronny Datcher to his holding cell.

Both Thomas and Detective Avery believed Datcher was a lone wolf and wasn't part of any hate group. They would still have to investigate further, though.

"I pray to God that this doesn't become our normal here in Charles county and America as a hold."

Thomas shook his head. "With all the things played out in the media, it's already the norm."

***

Marcia, Jada, and Lisa held hands while standing outside James' hospital room. They were just given the okay to see him. Jada was trying her hardest to be strong, but the tears still fell. Lisa's face was dry, but her palms were sweaty. She wouldn't be okay until she saw her baby brother with her own eyes; see him look at her and talk to her and annoy her like he loved to do. Only then would she be okay. Marcia was resting in faith that her son would survive his worst day. She couldn't wait until the day he would be released. But for now, she was happy the doctors had confidence in his recovery.

"Hey, big brother," Jada said, standing next to James' bed. They were shocked to see his eyes open when they walked in. He looked groggy, but he was alert.

"Hey, Shrimp," he croaked. His throat was dry.

Jada smiled, wiping the tears from her eyes. "Don't you ever scare us like that again!" She slapped him on the chest, forgetting he was injured. James groaned.

Lisa and Marcia gasped.

"Oh, I'm sorry, James," Jada said.

"It's okay. But, yeah, I won't scare you guys like that again."

"Was that your way of trying to get me to stay and not go away to college?" Lisa joked.

James grinned. "You wish. I'm taking your room; it's the biggest after moms. Of course, I want you gone," he weakly replied.

Marcia leaned over, kissing James on the forehead. "I love you, son. From what I understand, you were a hero. You saved someone's life."

Less than an hour later, James was peacefully sleeping. He had needed more pain medicine that put him right to sleep. Marcia and the girls talked among themselves with the television on low.

"Mom!" Lisa called out. "You're not going to believe this, but a pipe in the upstairs bathroom broke and water leaked on to the kitchen ceiling. It took me forever to clean up the water in the bathroom."

Marcia groaned. When she got them from the house earlier, she didn't go inside. She blew the horn and waited for them to come out. She could only imagine the mess in the kitchen and bathroom.

"Okay. We're going to have to get cousin Anthony to do the repairs. Call him."

About eight years ago, Anthony lived with Marcia for a few months. She was helping him out with a place to stay, and he was great at fixing things around the house. When Lisa heard her mom say, Anthony, she put her head down, remaining quiet.

"Did you hear me, Lisa? Call Anthony."

"I'm not calling Anthony. You call him."

Marcia was taken aback by her daughter's attitude. "Lisa, what in the world is wrong with you?"

"Nothing!" Lisa yelled. She got up and left the room.

Marcia's jaw dropped at Lisa retreating.

Marcia didn't understand what just happened with Lisa. Why did she act that way? *This has been a crazy day!* Marcia realized how tired she was both emotionally and physically.

"What was that?" Jada asked her mom.

Marcia shook her head.

Moments later, there was a soft knock on the door; then, Thomas entered.

"Hey, you're back." Marcia stood up and met him by the door.

"Yeah, I just wanted to check on him and you. But also, as the detective on the case, I have to ask him a few questions."

"Thanks. He's knocked out from the pain meds, but he's doing good. It will probably be better to get a report from him tomorrow." Marcia turned to Jada. "Jada, this is Detective Thomas. Thomas, this is my youngest, Jada."

"Oh, you're the guy Mom was looking nice for that day at court," Jada sassed, giving him a wave.

Thomas chuckled. Marcia shot daggers at Jada, who just smirked in return.

"I think I saw your other daughter Lisa leaving. Are you two heading out soon, too?"

Marcia turned to him. "What? Lisa left?"

"I saw a woman who looks like her driving off in your car."

What is going on with her? "Thomas, I feel like I'm always asking you for favors, but can you take us home?"

"Sure, that won't be a problem."

Before they left, Jada and Marcia whispered their goodbyes to James, promising to see him tomorrow.

This day has been a nightmare! Her son got shot and could have died, but what equally bothered Marcia was what happened with Lisa. She couldn't figure it out. Entering the kitchen, she noticed the ceiling damage Lisa was talking about but decided to deal with that later.

Marcia opened Lisa's bedroom door and saw her sound asleep.

Really?

She may have been pretending, but honestly, Marcia was drained. She softly closed the door and went to her bedroom. After a hot shower, Marcia climbed in bed. As tired as she was, she couldn't sleep. Her mind was racing. She stared at the ceiling. *James was shot. Lisa flipped out on me. My bathroom pipe and kitchen ceiling are a mess.*

Marcia must have fallen asleep at some point because she pitched up from hearing loud screaming. She scrambled out of bed. Standing in the doorway to her bedroom, she noticed the sound coming from Lisa's room.

"No! No! Get off of me!"

Marcia ran into the bedroom. Lisa was in bed, fitfully sleeping. Marcia tried to wake her up. "Lisa," she called, shaking her. "Lisa, sweetie, wake up. Wake up."

Lisa's screams stopped. Opening her eyes, she started to calm down. "Mom, I had a nightmare. Thank God, it was only a dream." She touched her wet face and pushed the tears away with her fingers. It had been years since she'd had a nightmare.

"A nightmare? About what?"

Lisa sat up. "Mom, eight years ago, Anthony sexually assaulted me, and I never told you."

Marcia's heart shattered. Her eyes snapped shut as she processed what her daughter just said. She slowly opened her eyes again, witnessing the pain on Lisa's face. "I'm so sorry, Lisa." Marcia gathered her daughter into a hug. "I'm so sorry." Marcia was kicking herself for not knowing. For not properly protecting her child. *How could this have happened?* "You've dealt with this all these years alone?"

Lisa nodded her head against her mother's shoulder. "I was scared. I was twelve, and he told me that he would hurt you if I said anything."

Marcia swallowed the lump in her throat. "How … how many times …"

"It only happened once."

Once too many. "I know you're an adult now, but never be afraid to tell me anything. Okay? Never."

"Okay."

They hugged for a long while.

Back in her bed, Marcia called Thomas. It was after midnight, but she didn't know who else to contact.

He answered on the third ring. "Marcia, is everything okay?"

"I just found out Lisa was molested eight years ago," she cried into the phone.

His heart broke from her tears alone. "What?"

"She had a nightmare tonight, screaming in her sleep. I woke her up. She told me her cousin I had staying with us for a few months eight years ago, molested her. At the hospital, she told me about the bathroom water leak and damage to the kitchen ceiling, and I told her to give him a call to help fix it. That's when she got upset and left us at the hospital."

Thomas was truly at a loss for words. "I'm sorry, Marcia. I wish I could promise prosecution for what happened. But with the statute of limitations, that may be a lost cause."

"I figured as much. But I'm going to expose him. This will not go hush-hush in the family."

"I agree. Keeping quiet only gives people, like him, the opportunity to strike again. I do think you should look at counseling, though. I know a great Christian psychologist. Her name is Doctor Lynn Calder; she's also a pastor. I will text you her info."

"Thanks, Thomas, my personal hero."

Chapter 10

"God created man in His own image; in the image of God, He created him; male and female He created them." (Genesis 1:27)

Have you ever wondered, what is your place in this world? I'm sure I'm not the only person who's ever asked this question. Journey to Faith answers these questions. I love the game show Jeopardy because the game gives you the answers, but you have to come up with questions. God, in creation, said that man was created in His image. The Hebrew word for image is tselem, which means copy or reflection. In other words, your purpose in this world is to reflect the image of God.

In this world, light is greater than darkness. If you were to reflect light into a dark place, the light would always overcome darkness. One of the greatest mistakes we make is that we sometimes compare ourselves to other people. It's like asking who is the greatest basketball player, Michael Jordan or LeBron James? In a sense, this is a silly question because they're both different players who played in different times. The key is not to be like Mike (lol), but to be all God has called you to be because you were made in God's image.

The next day, Marcia was able to get an appointment to meet with the therapist and pastor, Dr.

Lynn, at 10 a.m., all because of her friendship with Thomas, and the first three sessions would be free. More and more, Thomas was proving he was godsent. Lisa was a bit hesitant but agreed to go to counseling. Marcia had called her sister at six that morning to let her know what Lisa confessed.

A divide had begun in the family; her sister refused to believe her, but that didn't matter to Marcia, she wasn't going to let what Anthony did to her daughter slide, especially now that she'd learned he was known for being around young girls unattended. *What grown man babysits kids?*

Marcia was struggling with sleep deprivation, low energy, lack of appetite, and strong feelings of guilt. Too much was happening all at once. Her son was shot, her daughter molested, and the dire home repairs.

Dressed and ready for the day, Marcia made her way to the kitchen. She found Jada sitting at the counter, eating a bowl of cereal. A thought popped in her head that made her nauseous. She sat next to her daughter. With her big brother in the hospital, she didn't want to add more strain on her youngest, but she had to know.

"Jada, honey, I need to ask you a question."

"Okay, Mom," Jada looked up from her cellphone.

"Has … ah …has anyone ever touched you in a way that isn't appropriate?"

Jada shook her head. "No, Mom."

"You know, you can come to me with anything, and I mean anything, right?" Marcia desperately needed her to know that.

"Yes, Mom, I know. Is James going to be okay?"

"Yes, your brother is going to be okay."

"When are we going to get the bathroom and the kitchen fixed?" Jada asked before digging her spoon in the bowl.

"Soon." Marcia endearingly looked at her daughter. "I love you."

"I love you, too, Mom."

Lisa and Marcia left the house after one of the moms from cheer camp picked Jada up. Twenty minutes later, they arrived at the counselor's office. After checking in with the receptionist, they took a seat. Lisa busied herself on her cellphone. Marcia noticed the magazines and books neatly placed on the coffee table in front of her and leaned over to find something to occupy her time. She picked up a book called *Journey to Faith* by Pastor Brent Nelson. The book appeared to be brand new, and that's what caught her attention. She opened it and read the introduction: *The word journey means to travel from one place to another. Or you could say, we are moving from one season to another. When we are born into this world, our mothers and fathers planned for our arrival before we were born. Everything about our lives, where we will be born, the name given to us, the clothes we would wear, the food that we would eat, and the place we would live had all been preordained.*

Marcia thought this was interesting and continued to read. *Everything about us, our height, weight, genetic makeup, genetic dispositions, was preordained. Everything we learn is taught to us by our earthly parents. They teach us our values, how to walk, and talk. They teach us how to filter right and wrong, and they teach us customs and values.*

The purpose of faith is to explain the meaning of our existence. You were not a mistake. When God created you, He had a unique purpose for you.

Currently, there are 7.1 billion people on the earth, and you have a unique and special gift God has given you to present to the world. Your fingerprints and DNA are evidence that each human being is similar but unique individuals. Faith tells you where you come from, who formed you, and who foreknew you.

Here are five questions you should ask yourself: 1. Who am I? 2. Where am I from? 3. Why am I here? 4. What can I do? 5. Where am I going? These questions can solve most of your struggles in life. Because if you don't know who you are, someone else can falsely define you. If you don't know what you were prewired to do, you could spend many years doing something just to survive, and you are here on earth for more than that. If you don't know where you are going, you will stay lost.

As soon as Marcia finished reading, Dr. Lynn's secretary said that they could be seen now. Before she and Lisa followed the secretary to Dr. Lynn's office, Marcia placed the book back on the coffee table. She made a mental note to look for the book online later tonight to purchase.

Dr. Lynn had been a pastor for fourteen years, and she was in her mid-sixties. She had three kids.

Like Marcia, she was a widow. Dr. Lynn stood to shake Marcia and Lisa's hand, greeting them with a warm smile. "Please, have a seat."

"Thank you for seeing us on such short notice and again, thanks for three free sessions."

"Oh, not a problem. I do have to pay the bills around here, but I don't mind offering free services when needed." Dr. Lynn shifted her eyes to Lisa. "I'm sorry for what you've been through, and I have to let you know your confession was your first step in healing. You will overcome this, young lady."

"Thank you," Lisa humbly replied.

Marcia reached over and grabbed hold of her daughter's hand, giving it a gentle squeeze.

"How are you feeling, Lisa?" Dr. Lynn asked.

"I'm ..." Lisa paused to gather her thoughts. "I'm relieved. I was scared when it happened. Mom had left to go to the store and run a few other errands; she took Jada with her, and James was taking a nap. I was in my room, finishing up a class project when cousin Anthony came to the door. He asked what I was doing, and I told him. I thought he would walk away, but he came further into my room, shutting the door behind him. He had been staying with us for about a month, I believe. I was never uncomfortable around him, but that day when he came into my room, something felt off. He sat on my bed next to me, asking about my project. Then he moved his hand up my stretched out legs. I pushed his hand away. He placed it back, this time more forcefully." Lisa fought back the tears.

Marcia was crying, too. She couldn't take another word but understood maybe her daughter needed to get this out. "He—he raped me and told me I better not say a word, or he would kill you!" She looked at Marcia. Tears and snot were running down both their faces.

"When he left my room, I cried. I didn't know what to do. My stepdad had died not so long ago. I knew Mom had Anthony there because she wanted to help him while he looked for a permanent place to stay, and he helped a lot around the house. Mom needed the help. I didn't want to add to the burden by telling her what happened, and I was afraid he would hurt her. I ripped the sheets off of my bed and threw them in the trash; then I took a shower and tried to pretend like it never happened. From that day on, I never wanted to be alone around him." Lisa looked at

Marcia and continued. "If you weren't home, I didn't want to stay if he was in the house. I always made excuses as to why I wanted to tag along with you."

Dr. Lynn passed them more tissues to clean their faces.

How was I so blind to this? Marcia internally fought her demons. *My daughter was raped in my home by my nephew, and I had no clue. What mother doesn't know her child is hurting?*

"Lisa, I know that was hard for you to share; thanks for your bravery. And Marcia, I could only imagine your emotions as a mother on hearing this from your daughter. Please, don't blame yourself or beat yourself up about this – neither of you. You both are victims. But you don't have to stay victims."

Dr. Lynn discussed ways both could move forward and heal.

"As a Christian, I know I'm supposed to forgive. But I've been struggling for years," Lisa said.

Dr. Lynn acknowledged her. "Forgiveness doesn't mean having or continuing a relationship with a person; neither is forgiveness a feeling. Forgiveness is an act of your will to release someone, but more importantly, to release yourself. Forgiveness is more for you. Here's something I want you to do while you're struggling with forgiveness, I want you to think of God's shield of faith fighting the enemy's fiery darts. Recite second Corinthians 5:7, 'For we walk by faith, not by sight.' Forgiveness is the greatest expression of being filled with the Holy Spirit, but it takes a journey of faith to accomplish it. This cannot be achieved without continuous help from God."

"I believe I can do that," Lisa said. "I'm not going to let what he did hold me hostage any longer. Just talking about this is freeing."

Marcia looked at her daughter with love and pride. *She's going to be just fine.*

Chapter 11

"Before I formed thee in the belly, I knew thee; and before thou camest forth out of the womb, I sanctified thee, and I ordained thee a prophet unto the nations." (Jeremiah 1:5)

God is declaring that before we were a twinkle in our parent's eyes, He foreknew us. This type of knowledge can only be accredited to the Maker of heaven and earth. God is the source of life, but He uses man as a resource to reproduce life. Our earthly parents produce sperm and egg that creates a baby, but God is the source of the egg and the sperm.

Adam and Eve were the only people who were made from the source (God created Adam from the dust of the ground, and from Adam, God created Eve) everyone else came through the resource, (a man's sperm fertilizing a woman's egg.) God is declaring that before our parents knew us, He, who is the author and finisher of our faith, the Alpha and Omega, knew our beginning and our end while we were in our mother's womb.

Think about this: when you were in our mother's womb, God knew every detail of your life. Your life was already mapped out by Him. God knows your beginning and end, but He gives you free will to live your life. You are not a mistake! It doesn't matter whether your parents were married or not; it doesn't matter if you were a product of rape, it doesn't matter if you were unplanned, God had a plan for you. When a woman is pregnant with a child, it is a miracle when you think about the life growing inside of her. There are three trimesters to pregnancy, and every pregnancy is different, but it typically takes about nine months for a woman to give birth to a child.

God told Jeremiah that he appointed him to be a prophet to the nations. I believe God has appointed each of us to do something. Do you know what your purpose is? I hope this book is helping you to understand and or seek God's answer to what your purpose is. You can only have true fulfillment when you know what your purpose is. You were prewired to accomplish something that would bring glory to God. Find your purpose.

It'd been a week since the shooting, and Marcia was excited that James was finally coming home today. Lisa and Jada were happy, too. Lisa baked him a red velvet cake, and Jada made him a card and welcome home banner.

For the past week, Marcia had received numerous requests from CNN, Fox News, and local station TV and radio stations for her and James to do interviews. He was seen as a hero not only in the community but nationwide. Surveillance clips from Walmart, showing James' bravery by attacking the gunman had been shown all over television and social media. Even President Johnson tweeted about James' bravery stating, "We need more young men like James Jackson. Speedy recovery."

With the assistance of a lawyer that reached out to her, Marcia and James put out a statement but had humbly declined doing any interviews. She, along with James, didn't want any further recognition. What happened in their community had brought an international spotlight to the small town.

The media was still relentless, though. The security staff at the hospital had been fighting to keep the media away for days. One reporter lied and said he was James' uncle just to get a news story. Maybe after his full recovery, they would decide to do an interview.

Marcia was assisting Jada with hanging up the welcome home banner in the entryway of their home. They had twenty minutes before they planned to leave to pick up James.

Jada stepped back to see if the banner was straight. "It looks good, Mom."

Marcia got down from the stepping stool and stood next to Jada. "Yeah, I think he's going to like it."

Marcia's phone vibrated and then rang in her jeans pocket. She pulled it out, seeing Thomas' name on the screen. Her face broke into a smile.

"Is that Mr. Thomas calling?" Jada asked, seeing her mother's wide grin. She liked seeing her mom happy, especially with all the difficult things she'd been dealing with during the last few days.

"Maybe," Marcia said, walking over to the couch to sit. "Good morning, Thomas."

"Good morning, Marcia. How are you doing?"

"I'm fine. James is being discharged at noon. The girls and I were getting things ready for him. Jada and I just hung up a welcome home banner, and Lisa is finishing up on a cake she baked for him."

"That's great news. I know you're happy to have your son coming home."

"I am."

"How are Lisa and Jada dealing with things? And how's Lisa dealing with the assault on her?"

"You know, despite the tragedy, this has brought us all together. I feel closer to my girls. We have a more open relationship now. It's funny; I thought we did before, but they have been revealing more of themselves that I didn't know. Lisa also joined a Me Too support group."

"That is amazing, Marcia. I'm happy for you all. God is taking you guys on a healing journey."

"I have to agree …"

"Mom, we have to get going," Lisa said, walking into the living room.

"Hey, Thomas, we've got to head out. Thanks for calling to check-in."

"Anytime Marcia. Take care."

***

Lisa drove as Marcia rode shotgun with Jada in the backseat.

"Mom!" Jada called out. "Will James need a nurse to take care of him at home?"

"No, and they wouldn't release him if he still needed major care. Because of the type of wound he has, he won't need physical therapy. He's been getting up and walking, slow, but he's walking a bit—at least to and from the bathroom. It will take him some time to get stronger, but he's young and will be back to himself in no time."

"That's good to know. I'll still be his personal nurse, though."

Marcia smiled. "That's nice of you."

Lisa asked, "Can he eat normal food, especially since I baked him a cake?"

"I'm not sure. He has been eating a lot of soft foods at the hospital. They'll let us know in his discharge instructions."

Soon Marcia and the girls were in the elevator on their way up to James' room. They would be able to take James home without incident. The media hounds had died down. His room looked like a botanical garden. There were so many assortments of flowers, plants, and balloons.

So many people gave him well wishes and blessings for recovery. They walked into his room, finding James dressed in the gray sweatpants and blue t-shirt Marcia had brought yesterday. If she didn't know any better, he looked as if he hadn't been shot a week ago.

James looked up from his cellphone. "What took you so long, Mom? I was ready hours ago."

"We're right on time. You're just anxious," Marcia said, walking over to hug him.

"James, how much are you going to pay me to be your nurse?" Jada plopped down on the bed.

Lisa looked at her sister, "Really, Jada? I thought you were doing it from the goodness of your heart?"

Jada smiled. "Yeah, but a girl's got lip gloss and Vans sneakers to purchase." She turned to James. "So how much? I will wash your clothes, bring you all your meals, and make sure you take your medication on time. The going rate for a nurse is $50 an hour, but I would only charge you $10 an hour as a family discount."

James, Marcia, and Lisa laughed.

"How about we barter? I will be your Uber driver in exchange for your nursing services."

Jada brought her hand to her chin in a thinking pose. "Hmmm, deal!"

There was a knock at the door, and the doctor entered. "How are you feeling today, James?" Dr. Patel asked, holding a tablet and an envelope.

"I'm ready to go home, Doc."

"Yes, I know, James, but I have to make it clear you are a very fortunate young man. I take that back; you are a blessed man. The bullet did not hit a main artery. I've prescribed you some pain medicine to take as needed. I want you to finish your antibiotics. After you're done with the antibiotics, I want to see you back in two weeks."

James slapped his hands with Dr. Patel. "Got it, Doc! Dynamite!"

Dr. Patel laughed. "I like *Good Times* also."

Marcia laughed. "It's a guilty pleasure of mine; that's where he got it from."

"Here are your discharge papers. Follow them to the T." The doctor handed the envelope to James before leaving.

Marcia and the girls gathered up James' belongings, flowers, and cards. James only wanted to take a few floral arrangements. The rest he wanted the hospital staff to give to patients without any.

A nurse walked into the room, pushing a wheelchair. "Your chariot awaits."

James frowned at it. "Do I have to sit in that?"

"You do. You're not ready to walk for long without it."

"Okay, whatever it takes. I just wanna go home. This hospital, the food, and this bed have seen me for the last time."

On the ride home, Marcia was feeling beyond blessed to have her family together in one piece again. They were laughing and reminiscing on good times. Her cellphone rang, showing a number from an Arkansas area code she didn't recognize. Before answering, Marcia excused herself from the conversation.

"Hello?"

"Hi, I'm calling to speak with Marcia Jackson."

Marcia prayed this wasn't a bill collector. She usually didn't answer unrecognized calls, but something compelled her to. "This is Ms. Jackson."

"Oh, good. Ms. Jackson, I'm Rebecca Cooper, a representative of Walmart Corporation. How is your son James doing?"

"He's doing great. He was just discharged, and we're all on our way home."

"That's great. I'm happy to hear he's continuing to do well. He's such a brave young man."

"Thank you!"

"I'm calling because Walmart wants to do something special for you and your family. I understand James is one of your three children?"

"Yes, ma'am, he is. I also have two daughters."

"Lisa twenty, and Jada fourteen, right?"

How does she know that? "Ah, yes."

"Walmart wants to set up a $50,000 scholarship fund for each of your children, a joint trust for your children for $50,000, and provide you with a check for yourself for $25,000. We are grateful for James for not only preventing one of our employees from being killed but also selflessly doing a good deed for the community."

Marcia couldn't believe what she was hearing. *God, this is a joke, right? I'm being Punk'd.* "Is Ashton Kutcher on the line as well?"

Rebecca heartily laughed. "No, ma'am, you're not being Punk'd. We will just need to get some details from you to get everything squared away. Do you want us to contact your accountant, lawyer, or banker?"

Marcia fell against the car seat in disbelief. "Mom, are you okay?" Lisa asked, noticing her mother's disposition.

Before continuing the phone conversation, she nodded. "Ms. Cooper, thank you! Thank you so much." Tears pooled in her eyes. *Jesus, thank you!* "I will have my lawyer contact you. Let me get your information." Marcia grabbed a pen and sheet of paper from the glovebox, then jointed down the information.

"Kids, you're not going to believe this." Lisa, James, and Jada stopped their chatting to listen to their mother. She told them about the phone call, followed by shouts of joy. They had to calm down so Lisa could properly focus on the road.

"In that case, James, I change my fee to $1000 an hour to be your nurse."

They laughed.

Jada continued. "So, are you famous now, too, because the president tweeted about you?"

At home, Marcia and Lisa assisted James out of the backseat. Their neighbor Mrs. Crockett saw them pull into their yard and made her way over. She was an elderly black lady in her late seventies.

"Welcome home, James," Mrs. Crockett greeted him with a smile.

Marcia was shocked to see her neighbor; she wasn't mean, but she wasn't overly friendly, either.

"I'm so proud of you, James. So very proud."

"Thank you, Mrs. Crockett," James bashfully replied.

"Can I help you all with getting him settled?"

Marcia smiled at her neighbor, "Thanks, you can help bring in some of the flowers and fruit baskets from the trunk."

Slowly, but surely, James made it into the house and was now lying on the couch in the living room. In the kitchen, Mrs. Crockett placed the last fruit basket on the counter. She noticed the drywall damage, then looked up to see the wet stains on the ceiling. "Do you have someone to help with the repairs?" she asked Marcia, pointing to the ceiling.

Marcia shook her head. "Not yet. A pipe broke in the bathroom upstairs and created this damage. I've been so busy dealing with James that I haven't gotten around to it yet."

"My grandson Kendrick is a handyman. I'm sure he can fix your pipes and repair the drywall. Let me do this as my gift to you."

Marcia looked at her neighbor with wide eyes. She became overwhelmed with emotions. She went to Mrs. Crockett, pulling the elderly lady into a hug. "You have no idea how much this means to me.

Thank you. Thank you for allowing God to use you in this moment of my life."

Chapter 12

"There are secrets the Lord your God has not revealed to us, but these words that he has revealed are for our children and us to obey forever." (Deuteronomy 29: 29)

I'm going to use a three-letter word that sometimes is misunderstood in the Christian community. That word is, why. God, why did my son have to die? Why did I lose my job? Why did my marriage fall apart? Why am I going through so much heartache? If God is good, why is there so much evil in the world? Why are there mass shootings? Why are innocent people being killed?

I know a woman with two children who buried one of her daughters five years ago from a drug overdose. Three years later, she buried her second daughter, who died from brain cancer. Two months ago, she went to the chiropractor for back pains; they took an MRI and found out she has ovarian cancer. While talking to her, she said, "God is good not because of my circumstances but in spite of my circumstances. All is well."

Trust is the highest form of our Christian faith. We don't understand all His whys, but our relationship with our Father has allowed us to look beyond ourselves. We can only see from our limited viewpoint, but God has an eternal view of all things from beginning to end.

Some believe asking God why shows a lack of faith. I disagree with this. Asking why is a part of having a healthy relationship with God. My fourteen-year-old daughter loves asking the question why? She is not being disrespectful in asking; rather, we are forming a relationship with questions and answers. Sometimes she becomes angry with me because of my answers, but I'm big enough to handle her anger. How much more can God handle our anger when we're upset with Him?

When you get a chance, listen to Garth Brooks song "Unanswered Prayers".

Marcia needed a moment to recoup and process all that happened in the past few hours. Mrs. Crockett left thirty minutes ago, James was settled, and soon she would need to figure out dinner. She was sitting in her bed reading a page out of the book, *Journey to Faith*, which came in the mail a couple of days ago:

Who Am I? When we were born, we were given a birth certificate. This certificate identifies who we are. It also identifies our citizenship in the country we were born in. Without this identification, we won't have full rights to that country. Jesus told the disciples in Luke 20:20, "The important thing is not that demons obey you, but that your names are registered as citizens of heaven." When we accept Christ as our Lord and Savior, we receive dual citizenship, here on earth and in heaven. A diplomat is an official representing a country abroad. So, we are representatives of Christ in this world. When we become a member of Christ's body, we must consider, like in the human body, there are many parts. And every part has a purpose; they all have equal value and must work together.

"Thank you that I am a child of God," Marcia said out loud. She flipped the page but was interrupted by a knock on the door.

Jada walked in without permission. "What's for dinner?" She asked, flopping down on her mom's bed.

"Did I give you permission to enter?" Marcia placed a bookmark between the pages and returned it to her nightstand. "I've told you to stop doing that."

"Sorry, Mom. I'm hungry."

"I thought part of being James' nurse was cooking."

"He said he didn't want grilled cheese, and that's my number one specialty."

"Hmmm." Marcia got up from the bed and stretched. "I think I'll get takeout. I'll let him choose what we're eating for dinner."

"Cool!" Jada followed her mom out of the bedroom.

James was stretched out on the comfy couch, playing a video game. He had his headset on, talking to someone.

"What do you want for dinner?" Marcia asked.

James moved one of the earpieces for the headset from his ear. "Huh?"

"I asked what do you want for dinner? I will run out to pick something up."

"I can eat some pancakes, bacon, and eggs. Can you get them from IHOP?"

"Sure." Marcia looked at Jada, "Ask Lisa what she wants from IHOP."

"Okay. I know I want the steak tips with eggs and hash browns. Usually, that's out of your budget, but since we've been blessed today, can I get it?"

Marcia smiled, "Yes, you can."

Marcia had Jada call and placed the order at IHOP, hoping it would be ready when she got there. Twenty-five minutes later, she pulled up to the restaurant. The place was moderately busy for a Friday night. There were two parties ahead of her waiting to be seated by the hostess. She looked around the open floorplan of the restaurant while she waited for her turn.

What caught her eyes was the infectious way a young Hispanic woman looked, throwing her head back in laughter. The woman was attractive, youthful, and her laugh highlighted it. Marcia felt secure in herself and her physical appearance, but this woman had her standing there in IHOP, doubting it. What took the wind out of Marcia was when she noticed the woman's companion. She stared. So much so that he turned and looked at her, waving. She wished the ground would swallow her whole. She quickly looked away, pretending not to notice them—him.

"Ma'am. Table for one?" The hostess saved her from making her grand escape.

"No, I have a to-go order under Jackson." Marcia could still see Thomas looking at her from the corner of her eye.

He's here on a date with a beautiful young woman. She must be about twenty years younger than him, and she's younger than me.

"Yes, I believe your order is ready. Be right back." The hostess stepped away.

Please, hurry. The high Marcia had earlier quickly deflated.

"Here you go," the hostess returned with the order. Marcia quickly signed the credit slip and started for the door.

"Marcia, wait." She heard Thomas calling after her. She ignored him and continued toward her car. "Marcia, please. Wait a second." He caught up to her as she was opening her car door. "Why are you ignoring me?"

Marcia looked everywhere in the parking lot but at him. She didn't want to look in his eyes while he said he was on a date. *Really, why am I even upset? He's been nothing but friendly and professional. It's not his fault I developed a crush.*

"I'm just in a rush to get this food home to the kids," she said.

"Okay," he didn't believe her but decided not to call her out. "I was going to call you tomorrow. The gunman who shot James is facing eight to ten years because it couldn't be proven to be a hate crime. And there was only one bullet in the gun. It, unfortunately, doesn't help that the gunman is saying the same thing the president is saying about making America great again."

"Unbelievable. If the president can't be found guilty, neither can the gunman for being racist. At least, he's going to jail, and I hope he gets the rehabilitation he needs."

"Yeah. I ahh also wanted you to know that I will be retiring from the police force. The woman I'm having dinner with is my trainee."

Marcia finally looked up at him. "Congratulations." She couldn't tell if he was excited about retirement or not.

He smiled. "Thank you! It may not be apparent, but I am excited to retire. I've been offered a position as head security for T. D. Forbes."

"Wait! You're moving to Dallas, Texas?"

"Yes. In three months, I will be leaving Maryland."

Marcia swallowed the frog in her throat. "Oh, that's a long drive away. I'm happy for you. What an honor to work with such an amazing influential minister of the gospel, I've always wanted to visit Potters House."

"You should come to visit when I relocate."

Marcia weakly smiled up at him. "Yeah, maybe."

Chapter 13

"Moses answered the people, Do not be afraid. Stand firm and you will see the deliverance the Lord will bring you today. The Egyptians you see today you will never see again." (Exodus 14:13)

The journey to faith is a step-by-step process. Sometimes the hardest thing to do is to be still and let God defend you. There is a time when you need to defend yourself, but there are also times where you are defenseless unless God intervenes. Whatever hardship you may be facing, and feel hopeless, God has the ability to change it. Moses is telling the people that when you stand still, and see God's salvation, He will fight for you. The word salvation is a mixture of many meanings. It means physical, emotional, and spiritual healing – complete deliverance. Today, if you feel defeated or discouraged, you don't have to be alone. Because you are not alone, stand still, and see God's salvation.

Heading home from IHOP, Marcia was struggling with mixed emotions. *Why am I going through this with a man I barely know? I have a crush on him like I'm sixteen. I'm glad Thomas isn't seeing someone else, but I'm sad he's moving to Texas.*

When she arrived home, Marcia realized she hadn't checked the mail all day and doubted any of the kids had. She opened the mailbox. There was a letter from Paul, one of the men who attempted to carjack Thomas and her. The return address was Jessup Corrections Facility. When Marcia got into the house, she sat down at the kitchen table and opened Paul's letter. Mentally, she muted the noise of the kids as they greedily opened the containers with their food.

Dear Ms. Marcia,

How are you doing? I pray all is well. I saw on the news that your son James is a hero. When I told my fellow inmates I know you, they said, "Paul, you don't know no hero!" Ever since the day in court, I have experienced a hope I have never experienced before. The fact that you forgave me and had compassion for me is truly a mystery. You said something to me that I have thought about almost every day. You said the God you serve is a God of second chances. Could you please explain to me what that means? I have never had a person tell me that before, and I have never been shown compassion and forgiveness in the way you've shown me that day. Could you send me a Bible, and maybe some other Christian literature? I love to read, and all I have is time. I would understand if you don't write me back, but I believe you are a woman of your word. Thank you so much.

   Warm regards,

   Paul

   Marcia hugged the letter to her chest with tears blurring her eyesight. *I've been crying all day; this has been an emotional day for me.* She placed the letter down on the kitchen counter, then pulled out her cellphone to order Paul a Bible and the book *Journey to Faith* on Amazon. After placing the order, her phone chimed with a text message from Thomas. Butterflies fluttered in her stomach.

   Thomas: *Hey, hope you got the food safely to the kids. I forgot to mention that Ronny Datcher took a plea deal and would be sentenced in a couple of months. I can send you the info if you want to be there.*

   Marcia: *Yes, food arrived safely ☐ Send info. I will decide later if I want to be there. Thanks.*

***

Today was the day Ronny Datcher would be sentenced. Marcia had decided not to attend. *The next time I go to court will be to get my marriage license.* She was listening to the rebroadcast regarding the sentencing. Marcia looked up every so often to view the small screen in the recently repaired kitchen.

She was busy cooking gumbo for dinner and feeling a bit melancholy because she was missing Lisa since she left for college a couple of months ago. School was back in session for Jada and James, and she was busy at work, too, as an IT specialist at a public school.

James had recovered well over the past few weeks. He had the permanent scar on his stomach that would be a constant reminder of his bravery. To mentally heal from the shooting, James and Jada also attended counseling sessions with Dr. Lynn. Marcia wanted all her family members mentally, physically and spiritually healed.

The scholarship from Walmart was a huge blessing because Lisa would be completing her last two years of college without a huge financial burden. The money they gave Marcia also allowed her to purchase James a reliable used car for five thousand dollars and cover his insurance, which was costly for a teenage male driver.

Marcia turned the gauge on the stove to low, letting the gumbo simmer. It was one of Jada's favorites. She let the kids rotate choosing the dinner meals every other day. She picked up the stack of mail on the counter and began looking through them. Marcia sent a letter, along with the Bible and a Christian book to Paul in jail a month ago and hadn't received anything from him recently. She hoped he received her package because it wasn't returned in the mail.

Her cellphone rang on the kitchen island. She hadn't seen his name on her screen in four weeks. They hadn't spoken since that night at IHOP. Marcia felt silly about the way she reacted from seeing him with the young woman he was training to take his position, which reminded her for the hundredth time that he was relocating to Texas.

"Hi, Thomas," she answered on the third ring.

"Hi, Marcia. Are you busy?"

She sat on a stool. "No. How are you?"

"I've been good but busy preparing for retirement and my move."

"I bet. I never did thank you for serving and protecting our community. And I honestly don't know what I'm going to do without you around anymore to rescue me." She allowed her vulnerability and interest in him to show.

He must have been taken aback by her comment because there was a brief silence before he responded. "You're welcome. And I'm always a call away if you ever need me, Marcia. My number won't change."

"That's good to know."

"I believe by now, you may know that Ronny Datcher got sentenced to eight years for reckless endangerment."

"Yeah, I heard it on the news."

"How do you and James feel about that?"

"James and I believe it is a fair amount of time. I just hope with the prison system being segregated that his racist beliefs don't get any worse. I pray somehow he's surrounded by people who can be a positive influence upon him, and he gets rid of his bigotry and racism."

"Prison is tough, but you're right, if he connects with the right people and gets in positive programs that are offered, he can become a better man."

***

Paul was sitting at the tiny desk in his cell, writing a letter to Marcia. He had received her letter, Bible, and *Journey to Faith* book a month ago but didn't have any money for paper, envelope, and stamp until now. He was grateful for small things like just being able to send a letter. Being in prison had brought a lot of things he took for granted to perspective.

Paul ended his letter, then fold and stuffed it in the envelope. He was starting to feel anxious. Not about the letter, but about finding out who his new cellmate would be. So far, he hadn't had many problems since he'd been sentenced. He kept to himself and spoke only when needed. He was determined to get out sooner for good behavior and wanted to use his time in prison to better his education. Paul had already enrolled in online classes for a bachelor's degree in accounting. He was always great with numbers. His late mother constantly said he would become an accountant. He couldn't think of any better way to honor his mother.

He didn't want to have a cellmate creating problems for him. Paul preferred not to have a cellmate at all. Heck, not to be in prison, period. But, of course, he had no choice in the matter. He heard the familiar footsteps of guards approaching. The soles of their shoes were different and more distinctive than the inmates. Paul stood from the desk and went to stand at the entrance of his opened cell. Two guards were approaching with a white male in prison clothes, carrying his pillow and blanket.

"You got a new cellmate, Paul," one of the guards announced. "Help him get settled in."

"Can you mail this for me?" Paul handed over the envelope to the guard.

"Yeah," he said before walking off.

Paul watched them walk away for a moment before bringing his attention to the newbie who had yet to speak. "I'm on the top bunk, so the bottom is yours," Paul said, stepping back inside the cell.

The new guy didn't move. He just stood there looking into the tiny cell. It was barely big enough for two people. He looked over at Paul, sitting back down at the desk, lips slightly curled up.

"You might as well try to get comfortable; there are no penthouse suites here," Paul said. *What's this guy's problem?*

"At least, you're not Hispanic," Ronny Datcher mumbled under his breath. He walked into the cell and placed his blanket and pillow on the bottom bunk.

"You got a problem with people of a different race?" Paul asked alarmed. *I don't need no problems with this dude.*

"Only Hispanics and other illegal immigrants. I had a black girlfriend in high school, so I have no problem with you."

Bet not! Paul regarded him skeptically. "I've been in here a few months with no problems; I want to keep it that way."

"No problems from me." Ronny noticed the Bible on the small desk. "You Christian?"

"Yeah. I gave my life to Christ since being here. There's this church ministry with Pastor Rogalski every Wednesday. It's changed my world and has been helping me cope in here. You should come with me next week."

"I don't know much about the Christian faith, but I got nothing but time, right?" He laughed. "I'll give it a try. I got eight years. What about you?"

"I got six. But hope to get out sooner for good behavior."

Ronny remained quiet. "Yeah, I want to be on good behavior, too."

Chapter 14

"The Spirit of the Lord GOD is upon me because the LORD has anointed me to bring good news to the poor; he has sent me to bind up the brokenhearted, to proclaim liberty to the captives." (Isiah 61:1)

I pray you never have to file bankruptcy. It stays on your credit report for up to ten years, which could make it difficult to purchase a house or a car, or even get a job. For some people, bankruptcy is a necessary evil. Without the protection of a bankruptcy court, you can have your assets seized, and your bank accounts can be levied.

Sometimes bankruptcy has nothing to do with mismanagement of funds. It can be caused by sickness, failing business, or divorce. As Christians, we must file for spiritual bankruptcy where we lay down ourselves at the mercy of God, exchange our sins for His righteousness, and become pardoned. This bankruptcy entitles us to perfect credit because we are now children of God and have rights to all of His inheritance.

Paul laid on the top bunk that night with his eyes wide open. It was past midnight, but he couldn't sleep. Ronny, in the bottom bunk, was surprisingly sleeping peacefully if his snoring was any indication.

Paul reflected on his first night in county jail after he was sentenced before being transferred here; he couldn't sleep that night either.

That night after sentencing, he cried in his cell like a newborn baby. There was an old guy named Victor; he was in county lockup for failure to pay child support. He was sixty years old and still paying back child support. He failed to make a payment, so the Charles county police picked him up once again. Victor had been in jail so many times that he had his own dedicated cell.

Victor heard Paul crying and came to his cell. "How much time did you get, young blood?"

"I got six years," Paul responded with tears in his eyes.

Victor looked at him. "Can I give you some advice? This will help you when you're transferred to prison."

"Okay, what is it?"

"The first thing is to never cry in prison. Ever! You can get away with it in county prison, but don't do it in the state penitentiary. People will think you're weak and take advantage of you."

Paul quickly wiped the tears from his eyes. "Okay."

"Next thing, never borrow anything from anyone. This can get you killed. Third, never tell what you see. This can get you labeled as a snitch. Fourth, stay out of gangs. This may be hard because you will be pressured to, but avoid it at all costs. Stay busy. Work jobs, take a class online, do something."

"Thank you; I'm listening."

"Never trust someone until they have proven themselves trustworthy."

"How do you know if you can trust someone?"

"It's like being in love. You'll know when you know. Now, here are things you should do in prison. Most people can't read or write in prison. They're illiterate. If you can write letters for people and read for people, this can make you important. Can you read, Paul?"

"I can read and write well. And I'm good with math," Paul replied.

"Great, now you have an advantage. Here's the next thing I want you to do, get a job in the kitchen."

"Why?"

"Because, in prison, food is like money. It gives you clout, and it makes you important. Also, find a way you can help the guards and prisoners get along. There's a proverb that says, 'Wisdom is mightier than strength.' If you can do this, you will have the ability to represent both parties."

"Thank you." Paul was truly thankful. This was exactly what he needed to know.

"You're gonna be okay, young blood. Just remember what I told you."

That occurred about six months ago. Tomorrow, Paul was scheduled to have a meeting with the prison warden. He wanted to ask the warden about getting a job in the cafeteria and talk about starting a study group, among other things. Paul took Victor's advice to heart; being a liaison between the inmates and guards would hopefully make things more peaceful.

The next day after only getting maybe four hours of sleep, Paul was up and optimistic about his meeting. It was awkward now that he had a cellmate. He wasn't fond of having to use the bathroom in front of another man. He pulled the thin mattress off his bed and used it as a wall when he relieved himself. It would be another hour before the cells were unlocked to allow him to take a shower.

Paul's anxiety spiked every time he went to the showers. *Even though I walk through the valley of the shadow of death, I will fear no evil, for you are with me.* Quoting Psalm 23 always comforted and provided Paul with the peace that God would protect him. So far, it hadn't failed.

Successfully making it through the valley, he was now seated in front of the warden.

"Good morning, Warden Weston. How are you doing?" Weston was a white man in his early sixties with a head full of white hair. Paul took in the large homey-looking office, with the wall art and throw rug near the desk, there was even a small couch against a wall with decorative pillows. It felt surreal sitting there; Paul had already gotten used to the gray and sterile interior of the prison.

"Good, thanks for asking. Our records show you've been at Jessup for about six months. I'm sorry this is the first time we have met. So far, you have been a model inmate, and I would like to thank you for your cooperation. So, how can I help you today?"

Paul was pleasantly taken aback by Warden Weston addressing him like a human being. A lot of the guards needed to learn to do so. "First, I want to start a study group. We have the opportunity to enroll in online classes, but a lot of the inmates still need assistance with completing assignments, and some inmates can't enroll in courses because they don't know how to read and write. Perhaps they can get the help they need in study groups."

Warden Weston leaned back in his comfortable seat, rubbing his hand over his graying beard. "Okay. I do like that idea. A lot of our troublemakers are the ones who can't read and write. I will see about making that happen."

Paul smiled at the thought of his idea being considered. He kept going while the going was good. "Also, if it's possible, can I get a position in the cafeteria?"

"You have cooking experience?"

Paul thought about it some. "Not professionally, but my mom was a great cook, and I learned a lot of her recipes. I'm okay with washing dishes, too, if that's all you got."

The warden regarded him. "The head cook said he needed some more help; I'll let you try it out for a while and have him let me know how you're doing to decide if you can stay in the cafeteria or not. It may take some time to get the ball moving on things, though."

Paul felt like he'd hit the jackpot. Still, he refrained from showing too much excitement. He didn't want his eagerness to work in the kitchen be held over his head for any reason. "Thank you, I appreciate it."

"Also, keep in mind, in the next six months, I may get promoted. It's looking in my favor. We could start something, but I'm not sure something like this could last. Every warden has their own way of running things."

"Okay, I understand. Thank you."

Back in his cell, Paul felt optimistic and prayed things would work in his favor. He found Ronny sitting on the bottom bunk reading a page from the book Marcia had sent him, *Journey to Faith*. Paul stood at the cell entrance talking himself out of snatching the book out of Ronny's hands. He had little in jail, so the little he had was precious to him.

Ronny sensed his presence and looked up. "I hope you don't mind. But there's nothing for me to do. I saw your bookmark in the book and started reading."

"It's cool, but I would prefer you ask next time." Paul went and sat at the tiny desk.

Ronny nodded. "I just got to that part about where am I from. Mind if I finish? I promise I won't destroy your book." Paul gave him the okay.

Ronny was genuinely interested in reading the book. He grew up in the church. He had no choice in the matter. His parents had him there every Sunday for service, Wednesday for Bible study, and all the other church activities in between. It wasn't until his junior year of high school that Ronny started to stray.

The summer before junior high, his parents sent him to visit his aunt and uncle in McAllen, Texas. Uncle Chester was his favorite relative beside his parents. Uncle Chester hated illegal immigrants were freely living near and around his hometown. He had a major disdain for Mexicans. "They are everywhere! They need to go back to their own country!" He would always fuss his disdain. Ironically Uncle Chester had a love for Mexican food and often indulged. But he would fuss and cuss at the workers whenever he went into a Mexican restaurant to order food. It's a wonder he never died from food poisoning in retaliation for the tongue lashings he gave out.

It didn't help that during his visit, it was reported on the news about a woman raped by a Mexican. A lot of Mexican gangs were also known for wreaking havoc on local communities. Ronny got beat up by a group of Mexican teens when he rode his bike to the store. They surrounded him on his bike, pushing him off, stole the money his aunt gave him for the purchases, beat him up, and took his bike. It was during this summer vacation that Ronny's hatred for illegal immigrants grew.

Ronny continued reading where he had left off:

Where Am I From? Joel Osteen has a story about a scientist I want to share: "There was a scientist one time, and he went to talk to God and said, "God, we can now clone humans, make life, take care of ourselves, and we don't need you anymore."

And God said, "Okay, that's fine, but I want to challenge you to a contest before I let you go. Each of us has to create our own human using nothing but dirt, and the first one done, wins." So, the scientist agreed and reached down to start making his human, and God stopped him and said, "Whoa, not so fast. Use your own dirt."

When God created man, man was a spirit and soul that needed a body for the spirit to dwell in the earth. Like an astronaut needs a special suit to go into outer space, and a scuba diver needs a special suit and equipment to go to the oceans deep, God created man with an earth suit for him to dwell on the earth. We're not just made from the dirt, but the one Who made us also created dirt. We are from the mind of the Creator. The Creator who made the heavens and the earth.

Since Ronny was reading his book, Paul picked up his Bible to read a few chapters. He had written to Marcia that he would commit himself to reading the entire Bible. He was in Genesis, Chapter 39, the story of Joseph. Like Paul, Joseph was sent to prison. Unlike himself – the biblical Joseph was an innocent man.

Joseph was sent to prison for being lied on and for walking in integrity by not sleeping with his boss' wife. This intrigued Paul. *I'm in prison for doing something wrong.* A verse stuck out to him, Genesis

39:21, "But the Lord was with Joseph, and shewed him mercy, and gave him favor in the sight of the keeper of the prison." Paul read the verse multiple times until he knew it word for word, without looking at the page.

Joseph was in prison, and the Lord was with him. Paul pushed the Bible aside, pondering. For the first time, he became aware that the God of the Bible existed and cared about him; this gave him hope and perspective. Paul wondered if it would be wrong for him to pray that God would be with him like has was with Joseph and give him favor with the guards and the inmates.

He silently prayed, turning so his back was to Ronny and closed his eyes. *I have messed up and have made many mistakes, but I want to accept You, Jesus Christ, as my Lord and personal Savior. Come into my heart and mind. Make me a new man.* Paul quickly shoved the tears from his eyes. *God, I also ask for Your favor and wisdom. Help me to be a positive influence in this prison. I want to be light in this dark place. I want to provide hope and healing. In Jesus' name, I pray, amen.* He opened his eyes. It was as if a light penetrated their dark cell. Paul became mentally and spiritually free.

"I'm free! I'm free."

Ronny kept his eyes on the words he was reading but sarcastically replied, "If you're free, why you still in this jail cell?"

Paul shook his head with a smile.

Chapter 15

"No weapon that is formed against thee shall prosper, and every tongue that shall rise against thee in judgment thou shalt condemn. This is the heritage of the servants of the Lord, and their righteousness is of me, saith the Lord. (Isaiah 54:17)

Why does God allow evil or suffering in the world? This question is one many people struggle with, being that an all-powerful, all-wise, all-knowing God would permit or allow so much heartache and pain. I am secure enough in my faith in God not to try to answer things I don't have all the answers to. But here's one thing I do know, choices have consequences – either good or bad.

You can choose to jump off a bridge, but you can't control the consequence. I also can't fully explain why some people develop cancer or other diseases; we all know someone who has died from a disease we find unfair and question God, why? When God created Adam, he was created a whole person, meaning no sickness, disease, or aliments. Which means this is God's perfect will for all of us.

We live in a fallen world, a world that has fallen away from God's will. When God created the world, it was perfect, "God saw all that He had made, and it was very good," as stated in Genesis 1:31, which means our world was created with no allowance for suffering and heartache. The world went from order to disorder when Adam and Eve

ate the fruit. It was then our world fell. God didn't intend for this world to be the way it is today. The choices we make affect others – either good or bad.

The mass shootings becoming so frequent have hurt many people. An individual makes a choice that results in painful consequences for others. Our love must mirror God's love, which is the only way we can eradicate hatred resulting in murder. Just imagine if everyone loved their neighbor liked they love themselves, the world would heal instantly from at least 80 percent of the suffering we face. 1. My children would be safe around strangers. 2. I wouldn't have to lock my doors. 3. I wouldn't be ashamed of a weakness because others would not exploit it.

Another six months passed since Paul entered prison, making it one year he had been behind bars. Having Ronny as a cellmate wasn't bad. They were surprisingly able to tolerate each other in such a small cell and respected each other's boundaries. Paul wouldn't say he trusted Ronny, but so far, he hadn't given him a reason not to. One of the things they had in common were their interests in the Christian faith, Paul more so than Ronny.

And they attended the church ministry with Pastor Rogalski every Wednesday. Paul went to glean more godly knowledge. Ronny mainly went because it was something to do, and Pastor Rogalski was allowed to bring snacks like donuts, coffee, and juice – the good stuff. Not the overly processed and watered-down junk they were forced to eat and drink in the cafeteria.

"Get up, Paul!" A guard called out. "Be ready for work in twenty." Paul sat up on his bunk, rubbing the sleep from his eyes. Work in prison was a privilege. He'd been washing dishes and doing food prep for six months now. He only made a few cents an hour, but it was better than nothing.

Paul got down from his bunk. Ronny grumbled from being awaken by the guard and from Paul climbing down from the bunk. He soon went back to sleep, right before Paul left the cell for the cafeteria.

Though he had to get up at the crack of dawn, Paul enjoyed the peacefulness of the prison during these early hours before the noise of prison life began. The men in the kitchen weren't bad to work with, either. The food they had to cook was terrible. But since Paul started making suggestions, the food had become more tolerable, especially when they had limited resources.

"What do you suggest we do with these to make something edible?" Cook asked Paul. They were standing at the stainless-steel counter with today's breakfast supply: fresh apples, grits, bread, skim milk, jelly, and margarine.

Paul looked over everything and thought for a moment. "How about fried apples? We can use some sugar in storage, southern-style grits, and use some of the bread and margarine to make some fried bread?"

Cook smiled, patting Paul on the back. "I like your ideas." He looked at the crew. "Okay, guys, let's get to it."

Ronny ate every morsel of his breakfast. He never had fried apples before, but they were a pleasant treat today. He wanted to lick his tray but thought it better not to. The grits with salt and margarine were the right texture and taste, and the fried bread had him in food heaven. This was the best he'd eaten since he'd been there. The other inmates enjoyed breakfast, too. Guards had to break up two fights over inmates fighting over the last serving of fried apples.

A couple of hours later, Ronny was sitting at the small desk in the cell, writing a letter to his elderly parents. They lived on a fixed income; frequent calls from him wasn't something they could often afford. He also had nothing better to do. He didn't have a prison job like Paul. It wasn't Wednesday for church ministry, and it wasn't quite time for time out in the yard.

The smell of prison was an awful mixture of urine, body odor, and stale air. Some days, it was more intensified than others. Ronny paused his writing when he heard the distinctive footsteps of a guard approaching. The scent of peach, strawberry, and honey mixed enticed his nostrils and had him sitting up straighter in the uncomfortable chair. He turned toward his opened cell and saw two guards handing out mail.

The young Hispanic, female guard appeared to be in her mid-twenties, with dark, long, and curly hair pulled up into a high ponytail, stood at the entrance of his cell. The scent of peach, strawberry, and honey intensified with her standing there. "I'm officer Diaz," she introduced herself. This was her first day on the job. "Do you have any letters to mail out?"

Ronny sat there in awe. He finally swallowed the frog in his throat and answered. "I'm not done with my letter yet."

Officer Diaz noticed the sheet of paper on the tiny desk. "Okay, you can mail it tomorrow." She reached in the mailbag she carried. "Here's a letter for Paul."

Ronny went to retrieve the mail from her hand. As she walked away, he was still mesmerized by her beauty and fragrance.

He stood at the cell entrance and watched Officer Diaz like a creep until she was no longer visible. *I've been imprisoned too long because officer Diaz is the most attractive woman I have ever met.* He shook his head when he sat down to finish the letter to his parents. *The most beautiful woman I have ever met is Hispanic and probably got in this country illegally.* But he couldn't get her scent and beauty out of his mind.

Later that day, when Paul returned to their cell, Ronny handed him his mail. Paul excitedly looked it over. It was from Marcia. She still faithfully sent him letters. He ripped the envelope open to find a letter, along with a picture. It was from Marcia and her three children. He smiled, looking at the picture. Paul had some Sticky Tack he used to tack the picture to the wall by his top bunk.

When Paul left to do something, Ronny curiously looked at the picture. It took a while before Ronny realized the male in the picture was James. The same James, who fought the gun out of his hand, and was shot during the struggle.

Chapter 16

"The thief comes only to steal and kill and destroy; I have come that they may have life, and have it to the full" (John 10:10)

One of my wife's all-time favorite movies is Coming to America, starring Eddie Murphy, Arsenio Hall, and James Earl Jones. Prince Akeem (Eddie Murphy) lives a life of African royalty. He has just about everything at his disposal, everything except true love. His parents planned for him to marry. He was betrothed to Princess Imani Izzi (Vanessa Bell Calloway), who had been trained since she was a little girl to have an interest in everything Prince Akeem liked. There's a scene at the beginning of the movie where Prince Akeem met her for the first time and asked, "What do you like?"

Her response, "Whatever you like."

"If I command you to bark like a dog, you would do it?" She barks like a dog. Prince Akeem wanted someone who truly loved him, not someone trained to do so. Prince Akeem left his wealth to go to America disguised as a foreign student, living in poverty, working at a fast-food restaurant, to find true love. Jesus left heaven, His wealthy home, to come into the world to express His love to a lost world. Like Prince Akeem, Jesus wants us to love Him before we receive the benefits of Him.

Paul worked all three shifts in the kitchen today, and he was beat. But he enjoyed staying busy. Thursdays were usually long because he didn't have Christian Ministry, study group, or online classes, and he always stayed at least a week ahead in his class assignments to make sure he kept on top of things. With the time he had to serve, Paul figured he would complete his bachelor's degree in accounting in two-and-a-half years.

Dinner was over. Paul was in the cafeteria, wiping down the serving counter. There were two guards at a nearby table, keeping watch on him and the other guys cleaning up. Paul overheard them talking about the stock market, which piqued his interest. He loved hearing about numbers. Paul looked over at the two male guards. Officer Cooper was a tall white man with red hair, and Officer Smith also a tall black man with a low haircut.

Officer Smith was casually leaning back in the seat like he was off the clock, shooting the breeze. Considering the kitchen crew weren't troublemakers, Paul understood the relaxed stance. "I recently looked at my portfolio, and I lost a lot of money in the stock market," Officer Smith shook his head. "What should I do?"

"Heck, if I know." Officer Cooper replied. "I'm having trouble with the IRS. I owe about $18,000. It accumulated over the last five years since my divorce."

Now wiping down the tables, Paul gradually made his way closer to them.

"Oh, man, that's a lot of money. Are they garnishing your wages?" Officer Smith asked.

Shaking his head, Officer Cooper responded, "Naw, not yet, at least. That's what I'm afraid of."

"May I offer some advice?" Paul stood a table over, holding the cleaning rag.

Officer Smith grinned while he and Officer Cooper looked at Paul like he was crazy.

"What kind of advice can you give us?" Officer Smith sarcastically asked.

Paul didn't let that bother him, though. "I've never owned stock…"

"Go figure," Officer Cooper joked with Officer Smith joining him laughing.

"But there are a few things you should know about stocks. You should always buy low and sell high. Consider long term trading rather than short term, and invest in stocks that offer high dividends."

Both Officers looked at Paul with stunned expressions.

"Thank you, I will take that advice," Officer Smith said.

Officer Cooper sat up straighter. "What advice do you have regarding tax debt?"

"The IRS offers something called an offer in compromise. You said you were married, right?"

"Yeah, I'm divorced."

"Well, that qualifies you for an offer in compromise, which allows you to settle your tax debt for less than the full amount you owe."

Officer Smith looked at Paul. "How come I've never heard of this?"

Paul hunched his shoulder. "It's public information. A lot of people with tax issues, unfortunately, get scared the IRS will take all their money when really if you go to them, you can work out a deal. It's when you ignore the issue and have them chasing after you that creates a problem. You can pay a lawyer a ton of money to set it up for you, or you can do it yourself online."

"Really?" Officer Cooper scratched the hair on his chin.

"Yup."

"Can you do it for me?" Cooper asked.

"Yes, I can. When I'm allowed in the computer lab, we can fill it out and submit it. You can enter all your personal info without me looking. I can walk you through it."

"Huh, who would've thought we'd be getting financial advice and help from an eighteen-year-old inmate?" Officer Smith asked.

"Actually, I'm nineteen now," Paul boasted.

The officers stood.

"Thanks for the help," Officer Cooper said.

Officer Smith patted Paul on his shoulder. "Keep dropping these gems, and I'll have to start calling you Solomon. The wisest man in Jessup Corrections Facility."

***

"What's up, Solomon?" Tim, a twenty-six-year-old white inmate, greeted Paul.

Paul's nickname, Solomon, had spread throughout the prison. He had become the go-to-inmate to solve issues. From helping to make meals more edible and enjoyable to spreading the gospel of Christ, tutoring inmates, and giving advice to guards – Paul had become the wise one to go to.

"I just checked my grade, and I passed my GED." Tim had the biggest and proudest smile on his face. He was sentenced to prison for five years for petty theft. He'd already served three years.

Paul dapped him; he showed Tim how to a while ago. "That's great, man. I knew you could do it."

"Thanks for your help. Now I can enroll in getting my associate's degree in computer engineering."

"That's what's up! You'll have your degree by the time you get out."

"That's the plan," Tim confidently said.

Ronny stood to the side, watching the exchange. He and Paul were on their way to the study room. Over the past few months, he'd been reaping the benefits of being friends and a cellmate with Paul for which he was thankful. Prison was a terrible place to be, especially for a man like him. Though he was twenty-four, Paul was green to the world in many ways. It wasn't worth this. He was forced to man up, whether he was ready to or not. Attacks against him from the Hispanic gang had been averted because of his association with Paul.

Ronny had been regretting his stupidity of getting high and taking a gun with one bullet to kill a Hispanic to rid the world of one. *Are their lives less than mine?* He shook his head in thought as Paul and Tim spoke. Reading the Bible and going to church ministry had been pressing on his conscious. It didn't help that he had a crush on Officer Diaz as well.

"Hey, Ronny and I were heading to the study room. I've got a lot more guys interested in tutoring and helping with reading and writing their letters to family. We'll teach them to do it themselves. I need some help. Would you be interested? You can charge them a snack or nothing over two dollars from the commissary." Paul wanted the inmates to become independent and resourceful. *Give a man a fish, and you feed him for a day. Teach a man to fish, and you feed him for a lifetime.*

Tim's eyes enlarged with joy. His family was only able to send him $10 a month because they barely lived from paycheck to paycheck. He worked in the prison factory, making license plates, but he could use the extra money.

"I'm interested."

"Good, let's go."

Ronny agreed to help with reading and writing letters for the inmates because without a prison job, he needed to do something. His parents left him high and dry with no financial support. They were beyond disappointed with his actions and hadn't even come to visit him in jail. They did send him letters for which he was grateful. He hadn't told Paul, but he had no interest in helping Hispanic inmates. Luckily, the three Hispanics in the room didn't want his help.

Officer Diaz walked into the room, changing positions with another officer who left for a break. Ronny smelt her delicious scent before she even walked into the room. He found it interesting that he was so attuned with her presence. He looked over at her. Though she wore the same plain uniform every time he saw her, she made it look appealing, and her hair was almost always styled differently in a ponytail, it was either low or high, in a bun or loose.

Officer Diaz loved her job. It was the one thing she was able to accomplish on her own without her family's influence. Being the daughter of the governor of Maryland, she had become an outcast to the family and intentionally kept a low profile. Her dad didn't like the idea of her being a correctional officer, but since Sofia Diaz turned eighteen years old, she'd been rebelling. She didn't indulge in any criminal activity; she just strayed away from her family's political and social clout aspirations.

She didn't like the attention being the first daughter of Maryland brought. It was too much pressure. Her two sisters may have enjoyed it, but she didn't. When she applied for this position, Sofia used her middle name, Amaia, on the application. At twenty-five years old, she finally felt she was up from under her parents' thumb.

"You gon' teach me to read the letter or what?" Eddie snapped Ronny out of his fantasy. "What did my girl write back?"

Ronny averted his eyes from Officer Diaz. The last thing he wanted was for anyone to know he was feeling her; he needed nothing to be used against him. He picked up Eddie's four-page letter and started helping him with reading the words.

"Aye, Solomon," Officer Cooper said to Paul. He indicated with a head nod for Paul to come over to him, where he stood by the entrance of the room.

Paul excused himself from helping an inmate write a letter and went to the door.

"The IRS accepted my offer in compromise. They reduced what I owe to $2500."

"Good news," Paul said.

"Man, if it weren't for you, I would still be owing $18,000 and scared to contact the IRS. And probably would've had to pay a tax lawyer $500 or more to negotiate a deal for me. I can't thank you enough."

"It's no problem, man. Glad I could help."

Chapter 17

"There is therefore now no condemnation to those who are in Christ Jesus, who[a] do not walk according to the flesh, but according to the Spirit" (Romans 8:1)

John Maxwell has a book called *Sometimes You Win, Sometimes You Learn*. It can be easy to live with regrets over past mistakes or decisions we've made. In his book, Maxwell shares an important truth about failure and loss. Learning from failure can be one of the greatest lessons we can give to ourselves and others. We can't erase the past, but we can rewrite our future.

One of the guys that work for me had done some time in jail, so whenever he sees a police officer, he gets a bit afraid. One day, witnessing this, I asked him, "Why are you nervous? You didn't do anything wrong."

He replied, "I'm so used to having a guilty conscience that it's taking me a while to walk in freedom." We, as Christians, must know that we no longer have to walk in fear as the Scripture above states.

Marcia leaned against the desk chair, closing her eyes. A ninth-grade student messed up the wiring to a workstation in one of the computer labs, and she'd just finished repairing it. It took her from eight that morning to complete the task, and it was now a little after twelve.

She opted out of eating in the teacher's lounge today. She needed a moment of peace. Working around noisy kids drained her. She often sympathized with the teachers. Marcia opened her eyes and took out a turkey sandwich, with plain kettle chips, and a ripe banana she'd packed for lunch. After biting into the sandwich, she took her cellphone out of her purse to browse on social media.

She saw several breaking news posts about the president's only daughter, Ava, diagnosed with stage one leukemia. *God, I pray for her healing.* Marcia silently prayed. President Johnson seemed to be affected by the news if his tweets asking for prayers were any indication. That itself had been a shock to many.

Having enough of depressing news, she began snooping on Thomas' Facebook and Instagram pages. Though he didn't post often, he had a public profile on both. It was easy to keep up. On the four times he posted, she saw a glimpse of his new life in Texas. It had been months since he left with no phone call, text, or email. She was too prideful to be the one to reach out first.

She also was protecting her feelings. In such little time, her feelings for him had grown with no reciprocation from him. With his good looks aside, his personality and caring spirit would have her easily falling in love with him. *It's probably best I don't reach out. He's been gone for months, and I still grieve his absence.*

Marcia clicked out of his IG page to scroll through her timeline. She saw a notification someone just followed her. She clicked to see who it was and almost dropped the phone.

Officer_T301 started following you.

Thomas.

Her thumb hit the blue "follow" button next to his profile name. Right after, she received an IG message from him.

Officer_T301: I see your phone isn't broken.

MarC_Jackson: The phone works both ways.

Officer_T301: Touché. Bishop Forbes is coming to D.C. in a couple of weeks. Can we have dinner?

Marcia wanted to leap for joy, but she refrained herself. This was exactly why she kept her distance. She kept jumping ahead of herself. After a quick mental pep-talk, she replied.

MarC_Jackson: Okay. Send me dates, and I will see if I'm available.

Officer_T301: March 14-17. I'll be free in the evening on the 14th and 17th.

MarC_Jackson: I will check my schedule and let you know.

Officer_T301: Okay. I've got to go. But now that we've established our phones work both ways, don't hesitate to reach out.

MarC_Jackson: Will do. ☐

***

Thomas saw when Marcia pulled up and parked. He went outside to meet her. She smiled wide when she saw him standing at the entrance of Red Lobster waiting for her. She chose the location. She didn't want there to be any presumptions about this being a date. That's why she suggested the casual dining facility.

They hugged briefly. Both admired the other before Thomas broke the spell by taking her hand and walking toward the door. He held it open for her to pass by him.

"How is Texas?" Marcia asked after the waiter took their order.

"Different." He chuckled. "But I'm adjusting to being in Dallas. The weather is good. The traffic reminds me of D.C., and I don't have to pay state taxes."

"I'll move there for that alone," Marcia joked.

"Yeah, it's nice keeping a few dollars in my pocket."

"How is your son?"

"He's good. Back on the west coast, living his best college kid life." He smiled. "How is James since the shooting? What about Jada and how is Lisa adjusting to college away from home?"

Marcia smiled, thinking about her children. "The last few months have been great. We're truly blessed. James is back to normal. I bought him a car, and he's loving life. Thankfully, he's been doing well driving and following safety rules. Jada is your typical teenager and freshman in high school and trying to drain my checking account. She wants her hair done, nails done, name brand outfits." Marcia sighed. "And she's trying to convince me to let her wear makeup. I didn't have this problem with Lisa as a teen." She shook her head with a smile. "Lisa was homesick the first couple of weeks in Atlanta, but after becoming fast friends with her roommate, I barely get a call from her."

"I'm happy everything is going well with the kids. How have you been?"

Marcia paused her response when the waiter returned with their drinks. She placed the straw in the glass and sipped her soda. "I've been okay."

"Why only okay?" After taking a sip, he placed his drink back down.

I've been missing you and finding it hard to let you go because, in my head, you were mine. "I don't know. I need to find a hobby," she said instead.

"I've missed you," he genuinely expressed.

Marcia blushed. She needed to know that. "I've missed you."

"I know this may sound crazy with me asking this now, but would you be interested in us dating exclusively?" It took moving away for him to realize how strongly he felt for Marcia. He'd been pushing down the feeling from the second time he met her, but it never went away. If anything, it intensified. Now he was living miles away in a different time zone and asking to date her.

Marcia was at a loss of words. She'd wanted him to express his feelings for her for a long time, and now she was speechless.

Thomas looked dejected. "You know what, maybe …"

"It took you long enough," Marcia cut him off. "Why did you wait until you are thousands of miles away to ask?" She playfully smacked his hand on the table. He laughed with relief, entwining his fingers with hers.

"I'd been fighting my feelings for so long. I've also never dated outside of my race before. And I also wanted to remain professional; add in the fact that I had some insecurities since my failed marriage. I just didn't want to mess things up."

"Do you still have those insecurities?"

"Not enough to keep me from pursuing you. I know I can't compare my last relationship with the one I want with you. And I won't."

"What about dating outside your race? This would be the first for me, too."

Thomas took in the differences in the shades of their intertwined fingers. "It makes me want us more."

Marcia smiled. "Me, too."

"So, it's a yes to dating exclusively?"

She nodded. "Yes. I've never dated from long distance before. I haven't been on a date in fourteen years since my husband died. This will all be new to me."

Thomas leaned over and kissed her on the cheek. Marcia bit down on her bottom lip, hiding a smile.

"I hope you didn't mind that?" he asked, afraid he may have zealously overstepped her boundaries.

She shook her head, indicating no. "But I'm celibate and won't be having sex until I'm married. If that's a deal-breaker ..."

"It's not. I respect that, and you. I'm a man of faith, too.

Marcia mentally exhaled in relief. "Great. I'm sure we'll find a way to make a long-distance relationship work."

I'll move back here if I must, Thomas thought.

Chapter 18

"Yet I am confident I will see the LORD's goodness while I am here in the land of the living." (Psalm 27:13)

The state of hopelessness is not having expectations of good or success. Hopelessness doesn't care about your age, sex, gender, or economic status – it affects all of us. It can be masked with many different vices, which we must be careful of like drugs, alcohol, sex, overworking, overcompensating, the list is endless.

What do you hope in? Some people have hope in the economy; some people have hope in their marriages, children, and jobs. Hope is like a foundation. To build something correctly requires a solid foundation. Everything around us is subject to change; we must put our hope in someone far greater than what we can see. That someone is the Author and Finisher of our faith. We must lean on His everlasting arms for true support and hope.

"You heard we got a new warden?" Ronny asked Paul. They were out in the yard, watching some of the guys playing basketball.

Paul plucked a blade of grass, playing with it in his hands. He had an uneasy feeling about the new warden. He'd looked up Warden Pratt's bio online, and from the last prison he was at, he had a reputation of being beyond strict. He restricted his inmates from many privileges. He treated his inmates more like animals than human beings. Warden Pratt left his last job after the guards went on strike. Paul didn't know how the food recipes, study group, church ministry, yard time, work pay, and many other things would change under Warden Pratt's rule.

Paul looked over at Ronny. "Warden Pratt is his name. We'll probably be introduced to him later this week."

Ronny chuckled. "Of course, you know his name already." It amazed him how Paul seemed always to be one step ahead of things.

Ronny's eyes ballooned with fear when he noticed the group of men heading their way. He nudged Paul with his elbow. Paul looked up and saw Raul, the leader of the Hispanic gang, and five of his crew members approaching. The men spoke rapidly in Spanish, eyeing Paul and Ronny. Ronny died twenty deaths in the short seconds it took them to approach.

"We need to talk," Raul said to Paul in broken English. He looked at Ronny, "Get away, slug." He gave Ronny a look of pure hatred. Raul was a short man but not one to be messed with.

Ronny wasted no time getting up from the bench and walking away.

Raul took the vacant spot next to Paul. "Él todavía está vivo solo por ti." *He is still alive only because of you.*

Paul didn't understand much Spanish and had no clue what was said but knew it was about Ronny.

Raul waited until his men stepped back from earshot. "I've got a situation I need your help with. Since I've been in prison, I haven't been able to send money and support my family in Mexico."

Paul nodded, picking up more grass, and playing with it.

"My daughter Cara is turning fifteen. I need to get some money to my family to plan her quinceañera. I have an account here in the states with some money in it and need to make a transfer to my parent's bank account in Mexico. I don't trust anyone outside to do it. I've heard and seen what you've been doing for the inmates and guards. I want you to go online and set up the transfer for me."

"You have online banking set up?"

Raul nodded. "Yes, but I've never used it. I was never into that technical stuff. I only have that one account for business for the lil handyman work I did on the side."

"Do you know your log-in information?"

Raul nodded. "I got it all memorized." He pointed his finger to his head. "I just need your help going online and setting up a transfer. I will owe you big for this."

"Okay. As long as you know your log-in, we won't have trouble setting it up."

"Thanks, amigo."

"Meet me in the study room after yard."

Before getting up and walking away, Raul nodded.

***

Today's dinner was another hit with the inmates: chicken wings with a barbecue sauce Paul created with ketchup, spices, and herbs, along with mashed potatoes that didn't taste like processed powder, and sautéed corn.

Paul was working the serving line. Most of the men kept asking for bigger portions of the corn, but to be fair, he always refrained. That didn't stop them from asking, though.

The hairs on the back of Paul's neck stood at attention when he saw who was in line next.

Bobby wore an evil scowl. "What's up, big man on campus, or should I call you Solomon now?"

He had changed since Paul, and he got locked up together. If anything, prison made him worse. Bobby was now head of the Black Stallion gang since the previous leader was released a few months back.

Paul stayed away from Bobby as much as possible. Their friendship was long gone. Paul tried to reach out to him about online classes and church ministry, but Bobby shot him down.

Paul said nothing as he served Bobby some corn.

"You're still that weak kid I met in school. You may be getting some clout now, but you'll always be weak. When the guards and inmates don't need you anymore, they'll turn on you, and guess who's going to have to save you again?"

"Next!" Paul called out.

Bobby mean-mugged him before walking away.

Bobby sat nervously in the visitor's seat in the warden's office. His legs bounced uncontrollably. A guard was at the door to the office, keeping watch. The warden's secretary sat at her desk, typing away on the computer. Just moments ago, she told Bobby to have a seat and wait.

Man, this can't be good. Bobby was out in the yard, playing hoops. A guard told Bobby he needed to follow him.

There he sat in the warden's office, scared of either being transferred out or put in the hole for something. The something could be a long list of illegal things he had going on behind bars. As the leader of the Black Stallion's, he needed to keep his position by not only putting fear in his crew but feeding them, too. Money still needed to be had even in prison. The Black Stallion's made money by selling drugs, cellphones, and carrying out hits on inmates for a handsome fee.

He was starting to feel like a lil chump with fear in his heart, but no man was completely fearless, no matter what he portrayed.

"The warden will see you now," the secretary's deep smoker's voice broke Bobby's train of thought.

He stood and winked at the fortysomething-year-old white woman before he made his way toward the warden's office door. Bobby remembered his manners and knocked before he was told to enter. He quickly noticed a framed Redskins' jersey of "Williams 17." Being a huge fan of the Redskins, though they haven't won a Super Bowl his entire life, he knew the jersey belonged to Doug Williams'.

As he looked out the window, the warden stood with his back to Bobby. "Have a seat, Bobby."

Bobby walked over and sat in one of the chairs in front of the desk.

Warden Pratt turned to face him.

Bobby leaned back in surprise. "Uncle Teddy?"

Warden Pratt took his seat at his desk. "Don't ever call me that while you're in here."

Teddy Pratt had just married Patrice, his girlfriend of fifteen years, a month ago. Patrice was also Bobby's aunt. She and Teddy had been together for so long; people believed they were already married. Bobby had grown up calling him Uncle Teddy.

Bobby nodded. "I didn't know you were the new warden."

"Now, you know. And no one is to know that we're related."

"I won't say a word."

"Good. I want on in on what you got going on."

Bobby arched his brow, then changed his expression to indifferent. "I don't know what you're talking about."

Warden Pratt smiled. "Yeah, you do. I just got here, but I know you're head of the Black Stallion gang. Their loyalty to you is more than just fear."

Bobby crossed his arms. "And?"

"And if you don't want me making things difficult for you, we can work together making money together."

"What you need the money for? You run the place."

"Exactly, I run the place now, and out of courtesy of us being related, I want us to make this money together. And let's face it, I can do it with or without you." Warden Pratt cockily replied, leaning back in his seat.

Bobby thought about it for a moment. Having the warden on his side would make things a whole lot easier. But he had to be sure the warden, uncle or not, was on his side. "Aight. Game."

"Good." Warden Pratt opened his desk, pulling out a cellphone. He handed the burner phone to Bobby. "We'll communicate using this."

Bobby accepted it. Already this collaboration was working in his favor. "I need something from you."

"What's that?"

"I want to work in the kitchen."

The warden looked at him, confused. "Why?"

"I can *see* and communicate better with people. Everyone eats."

The warden nodded in agreement. "It is overcrowded in the kitchen. I had plans to cut back on workers. I heard the inmate Paul has been doing good things in there."

Bobby grunted at the mention of Paul's name. He couldn't wait to cut him down a peg or two. "Yeah, good ole Paul. Keep him on if you want. But I want to work in there. Work your magic."

"Done."

Chapter 19

"For the vision is yet for the appointed time; it testifies about the end and will not lie. Though it delays, wait for it, since it will certainly come and not be late." (Habakkuk 2:3)

When my wife was pregnant with our second child, she experienced labor pain she hadn't with our first child. The pain was so unbearable for her; she admitted that she wanted to die. "I'm ready to see Jesus," she said when a wave of pain hit her. Often, our greatest blessings are preceded by a season of darkness. There is a difference between burying something and planting something.

For instance, if you put a rock in the ground, it will not grow. But when you put an acorn in the ground and water it, the darkness in the ground and moisture will help it to grow. Some of you may feel like a rock – like your life doesn't matter, and God has forgotten about you. You must remember you aren't forgotten and the seed God has put within you will truly come to past if you remain faithful and remember who He is – a Promise Keeper.

The crew in the kitchen was reduced from fifteen to eight for each shift. There was more of a workload, but Paul was thankful he kept his position. He didn't like that a lot of the men he worked well with had to leave. He certainly didn't like that Bobby was now part of the crew. And they were always on the same shift. Paul had his suspicions about how Bobby got on in the kitchen, but he kept it to himself.

"Get your head out of the cloud, Solomon." Bobby purposely bumped into Paul, where he stood at the sink, rinsing off pans. "You don't want to be known for slacking on the job."

As he picked up the baking pan that slipped out of his hand into the sink, Paul held his tongue. For the past two months, Bobby had been working in the kitchen; he'd been trying to bait Paul into a fight. Bumping into him, making snide remarks, messing up ingredients, so Paul took the blame.

One time, Paul was pouring hot grits into a serving pan, and Bobby walked by, kicking Paul's leg and almost causing him to fall face-first into the hot grits. Paul sustained some burns on his elbow and forearm that blocked his face from getting scarred. Still, Paul refused to take the bait, but he didn't know how much of this he could continue to take.

When Bobby walked into the storage room, Cook went over to Paul. "I wish I could get rid of him. I've talked to the warden about all the mess he's making around here, but he won't budge on letting him go."

"It's okay, Cook, I can handle him."

"That boy is no good. And the warden doesn't seem to care," Cook whispered. He wanted Bobby out of his kitchen, but he was no fool. Bobby was head of the Black Stallion's and could make life even more difficult for him living behind bars.

"You shouldn't complain to the warden about him anymore. The last thing you want is problems from Bobby if he finds out," Paul voiced Cook's fears. "I can handle it. If not, I'll just leave."

Cook shook his head. "I don't want you to stop working the kitchen. I may be head cook, but the food has been better since you've been working in here."

Bobby returned from the storage room. "Break it up, Dumb and Dumber. Time to get the food ready to serve for lunch."

Cook sneered at Bobby as he walked away.

At his station serving beans, Paul noticed Bobby discreetly sliding something from under the tray of an inmate in line waiting to get served potatoes. These exchanges went on a few more times during lunch. This was something Paul had witnessed many times since Bobby started working in the kitchen.

Raul and his crew peeped what was going on, too. "The Black Stallions are taking our business. We ruled the drug game in here. His products are coming in way too fast since he's been working in the kitchen." Raul was shooting daggers to the side of Bobby's head.

"I heard he's got a guard or someone higher up working with him," one of Raul's guys said.

"Don't matter. He'll be dealt with," Raul promised.

***

"Can you save me some fried apples?" Ronny asked Paul. "Those are my favorite."

Paul yawned. He needed to get ready for the guard coming to escort him to the kitchen for work.

"Yeah," he replied, wiping the sleep from his eyes. "Why are you up so early?"

"I couldn't sleep."

Paul got down from his bunk.

"What do you think about Officer Diaz?" Ronny asked.

"She seems nice."

Ronny didn't respond right away, and Paul went about brushing his teeth.

Lying on his back, looking up at the ceiling, Ronny confessed, "I have a crush on her."

Paul laughed. "Okay. I think you're not the only one."

"She's Hispanic."

"Yeah, I figured as much."

"I hate Hispanics." Ronny sat up in the bed. "And I know I shouldn't. What happened to me as a child when a group of Hispanics beat me up shouldn't have caused me to hate an entire race of people. It didn't help that I had my uncle in my ear, feeding the hatred."

"Forgive. Release. Move on. You're in jail because of a botched attempt to kill a Hispanic. Whether you were high on drugs or not, it was stupid. And I know you can admit it wasn't worth getting eight years. Since we've been cellmates, you seem like a cool guy. I guess I can say we're friends. I'm a black man who has had to deal with people treating me bad just because of the color of my skin. As your friend, I can tell you it ain't cool. It isn't fair. And my skin tone doesn't make me any different from you or any other race. We are all God's people. None of us are perfect, and none of us are superior to the other. Let go of the anger because if your sitting here isn't a wakeup call, I don't know what is."

Ronny nodded in agreement and repentance.

"I think it's interesting you're attracted to a woman who's a race you claim to hate. That tells me God is working on you."

In the kitchen, Paul was in the storage room, removing the ingredients needed to prepare breakfast.

Officer Cooper walked in. *"Solomon,* I hate to be the bearer of bad news, but you were reassigned to janitorial duties."

Paul thought he was joking. "Yeah, right."

"I'm serious. I don't know why you've been reassigned, but that's what the work schedule said. You're on bathroom duty."

Paul's nose scrunched up. "Cleaning toilets?" *This can't be true.*

"I can speak to the warden if you want to find out why, but right now, you need to get over there."

Bobby overheard the conversation from where he stood, filling a bin with apples. "Bye, bye, Solomon. I'll be sure to leave the bathrooms extra dirty for you."

Right then, a rush of guards with a dog followed by Warden Pratt came barreling into the storage room. The kitchen crew and Officer Cooper looked on in surprise.

"We've been notified that there has been some drug activity going on in the kitchen. We're doing a sweep," Warden Pratt announced.

The large dog tugged on the leash to be set free. His nose was pointed toward the lockers, where the kitchen crew kept personal items and a change of clothes.

"Do your job, Bailey," said the guard holding the dog leash, loosening his hold so the dog could freely roam.

The entire kitchen crew was patted down; then, the guards and dog searched the kitchen and storage room. Bailey was relentless about sniffing the lockers. Locker A9 was met with a growl from the dog. The guard opened it and found a dime bag of weed.

"Who does this locker belong to?" Warden Pratt asked.

"Mine," Paul said, stepping forward. He looked over at Bobby, who had a Cheshire cat grin. "But those items don't belong to me."

Cook and the rest of the kitchen crew looked on in disbelief. Even the guards were shocked.

"Only you and staff know the code to your locker. I don't think any of the guards would risk their jobs for this, which means the culprit could only be you."

"Believe what you must, but those items don't belong to me," Paul adamantly stated.

Paul was placed in the hole for three weeks. He felt hell couldn't be much worst. This was not what he meant when he prayed to God that he wanted to be like Joseph.

He believed Bobby planted the drugs in his locker, but he had no way of proving it. To make matters worse, Paul knew Warden Pratt was Bobby's uncle, and the two had to be working together.

Jesus, help me!

"I can't keep him in there for long," Warden Pratt whispered. He and Bobby were in the kitchen's storage room. The staff had left for the evening.

"Why not?"

"A tiny bag of weed isn't enough to keep him in solitary confinement indefinitely. You should have planted more. And why didn't you put the cellphone in there?"

"A cellphone always comes in handy. I didn't want to give that up. And I didn't want to get rid of too much product, either."

"Besides, he has an excellent record, many of the guards vouch for him. I may be the warden, but I still have rules to follow."

"Fine. Let him out. He's no longer in the kitchen, so I'm cool with that."

Before speaking, Warden Pratt looked over his shoulders. "Some product is coming in tomorrow with the food delivery. Make sure you're here at five when the dry goods arrives."

"When are you putting more money on my books?"

"You will see it there tomorrow. Make sure you're here at five."

"Got it."

Officer Diaz quietly tiptoed away from the storage room door. She couldn't believe what she heard. She knew the prison system was corrupt. To overhear the warden being a part of it made her shake her head in disbelief.

Officer Diaz hid her smile when Paul walked out of the minuscule cell. His hair had grown out; his chin was scruffy and in desperate need of a shave. More so now than before, she felt he didn't deserve to be in there. None of the guards believed the drugs belonged to Paul. However, their hands were tied. She was thankful the warden finally decided to release him.

She placed cuffs on his outstretched wrists. He would have to wear them until she and the other guard escorted him back to his cell. She whispered to Paul, "I'm going to help you get some of your privileges back."

Paul gave her a weak smile. "Thank you. I'm just glad to be out of there."

Chapter 20

"Remember the former things, those of long ago; I am God, and there is no other; I am God, and there is none like me. I make known the end from the beginning, from ancient times, what is still to come. I say, My purpose will stand, and I will do all that I please." (Isaiah 46:9-10)

I recently heard a message in church entitled, Are You Stuck Struggling with the Promises of God? Whenever God makes a promise to someone, there's seed, time, and harvest. God told Joseph when he was seventeen that his brothers would bow to him; God didn't tell him that he would be betrayed by his brothers, sold to Potiphar, lied on, and thrown into prison. God is still faithful to His word even though the circumstances look contrary to what God said.

He is not just a God of time, but a God of timing. He is engineering our lives to be consistent with His plan even when we don't see it. Anyone who has done anything great for God has been through a season of silence (time). It took Joseph from the age of seventeen to thirty to see the fulfillment of God's purpose accomplished.

I don't know what you're facing today, but if you feel stuck, God is faithful, and His purpose will stand if you continue to trust in Him and not what you see or feel.

"Dinner went well." Marcia smiled. She and Thomas held hands while taking the steps down toward the Awakening statue located at National Harbor in Prince George County, Maryland.

"I think so, too. They got along well." Thomas chuckled. "It seems they're all excited about us being together."

Marcia laughed. "Ha. You think so? Jada got mad that dinner wasn't a proposal."

With school on a break, Thomas and Marcia arranged a dinner for their children to meet. Karter flew in from California; Lisa flew in town from Atlanta, and Thomas arrived back in Maryland a couple of days ago.

While still holding hands, the couple found a spot and sat near the statue. "I love her personality. She's definitely the baby," Thomas said.

"And she knows it and uses her status as the youngest to her advantage." Marcia smiled.

They were quiet for a moment, enjoying each other's company and taking in the people and view of the Potomac River in front of them.

Thomas turned, slightly taking in the side profile of Marcia's face. He was always in awe of her beauty. He'd been the happiest since they'd officially started dating months ago. Dating long distance was tough because he didn't like not being able to see her in person every day. Somehow, they'd been making it work. He had more flexibility than she did; he was able to travel to Maryland to see her. She flew to Dallas to visit him once. He enjoyed seeing the excitement on her face when he took her sightseeing since it was her first time in Dallas. They knew soon they would have to figure out a permanent location for them because it was tough on them being apart.

"I love you," Thomas said the words he'd been feeling for a long time. His heart picked up speed in his chest, waiting for her response.

Marcia turned to face him. Her eyes lit up with joy. "I love you." She threw her arms around his neck and pressed her lips against his. "So much." She pulled away from his face.

Thomas placed his arm around her shoulder; she laid her head in the crook of his arm. "I haven't proposed yet or anything and I promise you I will. I want us to start premarital counseling. I found someone that can meet with us remotely online."

"That's a great idea. I was going to ask you about that. At our age, if this doesn't lead to marriage, it's a waste of my time."

"I agree. Also, I've been thinking about moving back to Maryland. My house here is rented on a month-to-month basis. I can give the tenants notice to move. I don't have to live in Dallas for my position. I'm mostly on security detail when the bishop is out of town. I can fly into whichever destination he'll be at."

Marcia sat up. "Really? You'll move back?"

Thomas nodded with a smile. "Yes, I can move back. It would take me a couple of months or so, but I can get the ball rolling."

"That would be great, Thomas. I miss you so much when you're not close by."

"I miss you, too. And I want to do whatever I can to make this relationship work."

"Thank you!"

Chapter 21

"He called down famine on the land and destroyed all their supplies of food, and he sent a man before them—Joseph, sold as a slave. They bruised his feet with shackles; his neck was put in irons, till what he foretold came to pass, till the word of the Lord proved him true. The king sent and released him; the ruler of peoples set him free. He made him master of his household, ruler over all he possessed." (Psalm 105:16-21)

Joseph was thirty years old when he assumed his position as governor over Egypt. He experienced thirteen years of heartache, but God gave him ninety years as a reward for his faithfulness. He died when he was 110. That means while you're still alive, God will reward you for your faithfulness. You will enjoy the thing you're waiting on to manifest itself. To be successful in public, you must first be successful in private. Joseph had integrity when no one was watching. He was successful in Potiphar's house the same as he was in prison.

Cleaning the bathrooms were the worst. But it was better than being in solitary confinement. Paul cleaned until the place looked spick and span. Like when he worked in the kitchen, he took pride in what he did.

He thought about Colossians 3:23-24: *Whatever you do, work at it with all your heart, as working for the Lord, not for human masters, since you know that you will receive an inheritance from the Lord as a reward. It is the Lord Christ you are serving.*

It was hard to live by that Scripture whenever he walked into the filthy bathrooms for duty, but he persevered.

It was Wednesday, and Paul finished his janitorial duties on time to make it to church ministry with Pastor Rogalski. He and Ronny walked into the room together, carrying their Bibles. Both went straight to the snack table for the Krispy Kreme donuts and coffee.

Paul watched Ronny place a pink sprinkled donut on a napkin, then poured a cup of coffee, mixing in a splash of cream and three sugars. Ronny took the items over to Officer Diaz. She looked up in surprise from where she sat at the entrance of the room, smiled at Ronny, accepting his chivalry.

She sipped the coffee. "This is perfect, Ronny, thank you."

Ronny walked back over to the snack table, wearing a proud grin.

Paul was amused. "How do you know which donut she likes and how she takes her coffee?"

"She always gets the pink sprinkled one, and I've watched her make coffee enough to remember."

"Okay, I see you," Paul said before walking away to find a seat.

After the group was settled, Pastor Rogalski continued the lesson from the book *Journey to Faith*:

Why Am I Here? *Every believer has an assignment to fulfill on this earth. When you became a member of the body of Christ, you were drafted into a spiritual war. You are a Kingdom citizen, and because of that, in the spiritual world, you are a threat to the enemy. You may not realize it, but the enemy knows how valuable you are. Satan knows that God has given you authority and power in His name for the sake of the Kingdom. You are here to bring healing, hope, and to reproduce God's Kingdom. You are called to make disciples for the Kingdom. Have you ever considered what would happen if there were no police officers or law enforcement in the world? There would be chaos. We may not agree with all police officers, and sometimes they abuse their authority, but without them, the world would be a place where* *only the strong could survive. The same is true in the spiritual world, without Christians being the light and the salt, there would be so much more bitterness, hatred, and malice. You are here to reflect the heart of the King and His Kingdom.*

Breakfast in the cafeteria was coming to an end. Bobby got a lot of product off of his hands while serving eggs. His books and a bank account on the outside, under a fake name, were looking fat. He hoped to have enough in the bank account to have a fresh start when he finished his six years.

The guards made the last call for breakfast before the kitchen staff had to start putting things away and cleaning up.

Raul slid his tray toward Bobby. "Hora de pagar." *Time to pay.*

"This is America; we speak English here, Mexicano." Bobby scooped up a serving of eggs, spat in it, then placed it on Raul's tray.

Raul looked over his shoulder, one of his guys stood inconspicuously at the entrance to the cafeteria, sliding something between the handles, locking it into place.

Raul picked up his tray and slapped it against Bobby's face. He hopped over the counter, kicking Bobby; they began fighting.

More chaos erupted in the cafeteria. Raul's gang and the Black Stallions were the main aggressors. Everyone else fought for survival or ran for safety.

When the cafeteria doors were kicked open by the guards, the blaring of an alarm, indicating a shutdown, did nothing to stop the riot in the cafeteria from spilling out into other parts of the prison. Bobby fought with everything in him, but Raul was overpowering him. The blow to the head with the tray still had Bobby dazed.

"You should've stayed in your lane. I run the drug business in here." Raul punched Bobby in the face; blood went flying.

Bobby jabbed him in the gut and pushed Raul off of him. "It couldn't have been yours if it was easily taken."

"We'll see about that," Raul replied right before Bobby stomped on his chest.

Paul took swift action in locking and barricading the room they were in for church ministry.

Pastor Rogalski stood in a corner, fearing for his safety. In all the years he'd been coming to the prison, he'd never experienced anything like this.

"You're going to be okay; we won't let them in here," Paul assured him.

Some of Raul's crew were banging on the door for entry. Officer Diaz and the male guard, Officer Rolle, in the room were on their radios, calling for backup and status on what was happening. All the two officers had for protection was pepper spray, they weren't allowed to carry guns around prisoners.

The banging on the door persisted. Officer Diaz and Officer Rolle were becoming antsy. There were nine inmates in the room, along with Pastor Rogalski.

The small window in the door was bashed open. Officer Diaz unwillingly screamed in fear. Ronny was immediately at her side. "I won't let anything happen to you," he promised.

She was supposed to be protecting them, and he was coming to her rescue.

In the cafeteria, Raul and Bobby were weakly on their feet; exhaustion was trying to get the best of them. Raul charged at Bobby, tackling him to the ground. He searched the floor, finding a chained knife hanging toward the floor. He reached for it, but it wasn't long enough.

Bobby used this distraction to punch Raul. He shook out of the punch and swiftly placed Bobby in a chokehold, dragging him toward the knife. Bobby's eyes enlarged in fear upon seeing the steel falling toward his chest. Raul punctured his flesh several times before he was sure his enemy took his last breath.

"We don't want any trouble," Paul told the men in Raul's crew. They stood in the doorway of the room. "We have no parts of what's going on with you and the Black Stallions."

"You don't. And we don't want you. We want the guards and the pastor. They're our ticket out of here."

"She's not going anywhere," Ronny spoke up, standing in front of Officer Diaz.

One of the guys laughed in his face. "Isn't this cute. You're a racist standing up for one of us."

"I'm not a racist," Ronny proclaimed.

"Since when?" Raul's guy asked.

Ronny boldly spoke, "Since God forgave me, and I repented. She's innocent. Don't bring her into this."

"We don't forgive you. And the only reason you've lived this long was because of Paul. Raul has respect for him, which flowed over to you. But I'm not feeling real generous right now."

With blood all over him, Raul walked into the room. "Cuff the guards and the pastor." His men moved into action.

"No, Raul, you owe me. Don't do this, please," Paul spoke up.

Raul shook his head. "I need them, or I will die or be placed on death row."

"You honestly think keeping them hostage is going to get you and your men out of here?" Paul questioned in disbelief. "This is real life. They're not going to take a prisoner seriously."

"They will with them." Raul pointed to Officer Diaz, Officer Rolle, and Pastor Rogalski handcuffed together.

"You owe me, Raul," Paul reasoned again. "All of this would most likely fall on the Black Stallions if you play it cool. Taking this extreme measure will only make matters worse for you."

Raul rubbed his chin, weighing his options. "You've been wise before, so I will take your advice. I better not regret this."

Paul sighed in relief.

"Let them go." The men followed Raul's order.

Tears stung Officer Diaz's eyes. She'd never been this afraid in her life. One of the men licked her face when he cuffed her earlier. Thinking about what they could have done had her beyond thankful for Paul's intervention

"Are you okay?" Ronny asked when the cuffs were released from her wrists. She rubbed them for relief.

She nodded. "Tha—thank you for standing up for me."

Ronny badly wanted to hug her but was satisfied by being close. "I wished I could've done more. But you're safe. They're not going to hurt you."

Shouts and footsteps were heard outside the room. A group of enraged Black Stallions came in, some with makeshift weapons. "Looks like the party's in here, and it's not going to end well for any of you."

Paul moved to protect Pastor Rogalski, standing in front of him, holding a chair as a weapon.

Ronny took Officer Diaz's hand, placing her behind him. "Do you have a weapon? Baton, pepper spray?"

She nodded, fearfully pulling the pepper spray from her belt clip; she handed it to Ronny.

"Stay behind me; I'll get you out of here," he promised.

Fights ensued, mainly between Raul's gang and the Black Stallions. Paul took the first clear shot at the door to guide Pastor Rogalski safely out of the room. Ronny took the opening, too, taking Officer Diaz's hand, guiding her out. Officer Rolle did the same while discreetly radioing in again for help and giving their location.

"Not so fast, Ronny." One of Raul's guys punched him in the face, knocking him against Officer Diaz. She screamed.

"Go, run!" Ronny said. She looked at him with uncertainty. "Go, please!"

"Listen to him, princess." He yanked her by her ponytail. "But first, let me get another taste." Raul's guy went to kiss her.

Ronny lost it and clocked him in the jaw. The guy barely budged; he was a huge man in comparison to Ronny.

Officer Diaz was released from his hold. "You really do have a thing for her, huh. Too bad, this will be your last time seeing her." He swiftly pulled out a makeshift knife, shoving it into Ronny's side. "Hora de irse a dormir." *Time to go to sleep.*

In horror, Officer Diaz watched Ronny fall unconsciously to the ground.

***

Backup was called in, and they helped get the riot under control. It made headlines on national news. Several inmates died. The Black Stallions were held more responsible because many of the deaths were by their hands. Raul and his gang would be in solitary confinement for a couple of months for their roles. Warden Pratt was also under investigation and placed on leave without pay.

The bed felt oddly comfortable and soft. The forever awful mixture of urine, body odor, and stale air wasn't present. The air was fresh. Clean. Ronny took a deep breath but felt a dull pain in his side. He opened his eyes and was graced with the most beautiful view.

Officer Diaz

"Hi," she said. "I've been waiting for you to wake up. Between the surgery and pain meds, you've been out of it for two days."

After he was stabbed, guards with weapons and body armor took over the prison. Ronny laid on the ground bleeding out for a while before he was transported to the hospital. Officer Diaz stayed by his side, adding pressure to the wound, which most likely saved his life.

Ronny started remembering why he was in the hospital. *The riot.* "Did…did he…hurt you?" His throat was dry.

She shook her head. "No. Right after you passed out, the guards took control."

"Paul?"

"Paul is fine. Pastor Rogalski is fine."

He nodded.

"I'm leaving. I resigned from my position as a prison officer."

Ronny looked at her for a while, trying to memorize her face. A tear slid from his eye. He looked away.

"Are you okay? Are you in pain? I can call the nurse …" She went to stand from the chair near his hospital bed.

He stilled her by grasping her hand. "I'm okay."

"Are you sure."

"Yes. I guess I'll be leaving here soon, too."

She nodded. "Yes. As soon as the doctor gives you the okay, you can go home."

Ronny laughed weakly. "It's not exactly home. But I have a few more years."

She shook her head. "No. You get to go *home*."

He sat up weakly, ignoring the pain.

She placed a hand on his cheek. "My father's the governor of Maryland. He pardoned you and Paul for your bravery in protecting me, the prisoners, guards, and Pastor Rogalski. You're a free man. I know you're not the same man sentenced a year ago."

Ronny shamelessly cried tears of joy. "I promise you I'm not."

"Good. Maybe I'll see you around sometime."

Ronny smiled. "Yes, sometime."

Chapter 22

"But Joseph said to them, "Don't be afraid. Am I in the place of God? You intended to harm me, but God intended it for good to accomplish what is now being done, the saving of many lives. So then, don't be afraid. I will provide for you and your children." And he reassured them and spoke kindly to them." (Genesis 50:19-21)

If I were asked what the greatest evidence of spiritual maturity is, it would have to be the ability to show genuine forgiveness. Forgiveness is not a feeling; it is a byproduct of being filled with the spirit of God. Forgiveness doesn't mean relationships will be restored. Some bridges are burnt and will never be repaired. But the offense has been forgiven. Joseph exhibited enormous faith in his forgiveness to his brothers. It was because of them that he suffered so many years in prison.

But in the end, he became the second in command in Egypt. He had the opportunity to punish his brothers and even brag about his new success, but he showed them mercy and forgiveness instead. For an electrical device to work, it must be plugged into the power source. For forgiveness to work, we must plug into the power source of God.

If you are showing symptoms of unforgiveness, could it be you're not properly plugged into the power source of God?

It had been a few days since Paul and Ronny were released from prison. Paul was living with his aunt until he was able to afford to move out. He was thankful he would be able to finish the semester taking online classes toward his bachelor's degree in accounting. He was already looking into scholarships and financial aid needed to finance college classes for the following semesters. Paul had some legit ideas for making an income while attending college; he was all for being his own boss.

Ronny was back home, living with his parents. He, too, had no plans of staying for long. He wanted to be independent and get his own place. He was taking Paul's lead by continuing his education. He was looking into a trade school to become a certified electrician. While he did that, he hoped to get a job as an electrician apprentice since he had prior experience.

Ronny called Paul to meet up for lunch at Buffalo Wild Wings.

After ordering hot wings and sodas, Ronny cleared his throat in attempts to calm his nerves. "I need to talk to you about something,"

"What's up?" Paul leaned back casually in the seat.

"That woman, Marcia, that you often received letters from. I'm the one who shot her son. Well, it was my gun that went off and shot him when he fought for the gun out of my hand."

"You thought I didn't know that?"

Ronny looked surprised.

"I Googled you when you became my cellmate. I know all about what happened at Walmart that day. It was hard not to know when you were plastered all over the news."

"When I saw the photo of Marcia and her family you had on the wall, I knew I had to tell you. I'm sorry for what happened to James and for being the cause of it."

"I wrote Marcia about you. I told her how much you've changed. Even though at first, you were a bit reluctant about church ministry and fully accepting Christ, you finally did, and you're a better man because of it. Marcia once told me that the God she serves, Jehovah, is a God of second chances. God gave me a second chance, and He gave you one, too. Marcia and James have already forgiven you."

Ronny sat back, fully taking in what Paul was saying.

"The Bible says all things work together for good. The fact that you were in prison wasn't good, but while in prison, you produced good. You gave your life to Christ. You recognized your hatred toward Hispanics and released it to God for forgiveness and healing. You developed feelings for Officer Diaz. You helped save not only her but inmates and Pastor Rogalski. If it weren't for you, Officer Diaz would've been assaulted or even killed, and she happened to be the governor's daughter. God gave you favor with the person who pardoned your conviction. John 15:13 says, 'Greater love has no one than this: to lay down one's life for one's friends.' You didn't act in bravery out of selfish reasons; you did it because you cared."

Paul picked up his glass and drank some soda. He returned the glass before continuing. "When I was in county lockup before being transferred to prison, a guy there named Victor gave me some tips on surviving prison. One of them was to find someone I could trust. I trust you, Ronny, and consider you a friend."

Ronny manned up and quickly wiped tears away. "Thanks, man. I wouldn't have survived if it hadn't for you. Thanks for being my friend. And can you call Marcia and ask if it would be okay for me to meet with her and James?"

"Yes, I can do that and let you know."

"Thank you."

***

"Are you sure about meeting them?" Thomas asked. Marcia was chatting with him via FaceTime.

She nodded. "Yes. You know I've been writing Paul since he went to prison. Then to find out God had him become cellmates with Ronny, I just knew God had a plan. Now they're free from jail for heroic acts of kindness." She applied lip gloss before stepping away from the mirror, heading to her bedroom door.

Thomas eyed her appreciatively. "Why are you getting dolled up to meet them?" he teased.

Marcia laughed. "Don't I always look nice?"

"Of course."

"Then me looking fabulous has nothing to do with me meeting them. The man I'm dating has already captured my heart."

Thomas smiled broadly. "I hope he knows how blessed he is, whoever he is."

"I'm sure he does."

"Tell Thomas hi for me, Mom," Jada said when Marcia walked into the kitchen, holding the phone up to her face.

"Hi, Jada," Thomas called. "I plan on being in town next week for your soccer game."

"Really?" Jada got excited and stood behind Marcia so she could see Thomas' face on the cellphone screen.

"Yes, really," he said.

"That means I gotta bring my A-game."

Marcia playfully smacked her forehead with a free hand. "You should've already brought your A-game. You do realize your team only won one game so far for the season."

"And that was the game when Thomas was there, which means we'll definitely win next week's game," Jada bragged.

Thomas chuckled. "I don't need that type of pressure. But I do plan on being there. My flight will be in a day before."

The doorbell rang.

"Okay, cool. Thanks for coming for my game!" Jada kissed Marcia on the cheek. "I'll see you later, Mom. Stacia and her mom are here to take us to the mall."

"Remember your spending limit and not to purchase anything I won't approve of. Have fun!" Marcia called out. Jada grabbed her bag and headed for the front door.

"Oh, boy, I have a feeling you're going to call me later about what she shouldn't have purchased."

"You can tell, huh?"

Thomas laughed. "Yup."

"Hey, Thomas," James said, walking into the kitchen. "Hi, mom, ready to go?"

Marcia nodded.

"Hi, James. Did you remember to put oil in you and your mom's car like I showed you?"

James went into the fridge and got a canned soda. "I did it yesterday. Mom's was really low."

Thomas groaned.

"I know. I know. But it's my baby," Marcia said, referring to her fifteen-year-old car. "I looked at the car options you sent me. When you're here next week, we can go car shopping."

"Finally!" Thomas and James said at the same time.

A short time later, James and Marcia walked into a local coffee shop to meet Paul and Ronny. The two men were already seated, sipping on their coffee drinks.

Marcia noticed how different Paul looked from the last time she saw him in court. Compared to then, he looked lighter and free – no pun intended. He still looked youthful for his barely twenty years of life, but with it was an aura of wisdom and maturity. She smiled.

Ronny looked different, too. Not like a thug high off of drugs and hellbent on killing her son. At least that was her thoughts then when James was shot. Now he seemed like a regular, decent young man.

"He looks different," James whispered at her side.

"Who?"

James whispered back, "Ronny. He looks better. I guess jail really did reform him."

When they saw James and Marcia approaching, Paul stood, followed by Ronny. "Thanks for coming." Paul shook James' hand. Marcia swatted his hand away, pulling him into a motherly hug.

"I thought it would have been years before I could do this," she said to Paul.

Paul nodded with teary eyes. "I owe you so much, Ms. Marcia. But most of all, for forgiving me and showing me the love of Christ."

Marcia wiped tears. "You're welcome." She turned to Ronny, who nervously watched the exchange. "Hi, Ronny." He held out his hand for a handshake. She swatted it away as well and hugged him tenderly. "You are forgiven. I'm so thankful you allowed the Lord to work in your life. Our God is a God of love, not hate."

Ronny nodded, pulling away from the embrace. "Thank you. I don't deserve your forgiveness, but I appreciate it very much." He turned to James. "I'm sorry you got hurt because of my actions. Thank you for stopping me from acting in hatred. I thank God nobody's life was lost."

"I forgive you. It's good to know you've changed. That means you're not racist anymore, right?" James asked.

"That's right. I no longer see Hispanics or any race different than mine as inferior. In prison, I went to church ministry, and Pastor Rogalski taught that from one-man, God created every nation that exists as stated in Acts 17:26, which means we are all related regardless of our race. A cat and a dog can't procreate because they are not of the same kind. But every human being, regardless of their race, can procreate a child together. This means we're all equal. I was taught how to hate and have prejudice. When I began my journey to faith, I learned to see myself, others, and our heavenly Father from a different perspective. I cannot say I love God and hate my neighbor."

Chapter 23

"Delight thyself also in the Lord: and he shall give thee the desires of thine heart." (Psalm 37:4)

Daily seek direction from the Lord. Take delight in Him working in your life. Take delight in following His instructions and living a godly life. Delight in the Lord is not about seeking Him for your selfish desires. It's about earnestly and wholeheartedly surrendering your will to Him and waiting for His timing to produce His promise for your life. It's you fully surrendering and not trying to manipulate the situation on your own. It's going to God, saying, "What is your plan for me?" Not, "Lord, bless these plans." Several things that come to mind when I think about the past, I asked God to bless my mess instead of asking Him to show me Your best. I could've avoided many heartaches if I had fully delighted in the Lord. Don't make the same mistake.

"I've been reading that book you recommended, *Journey to Faith*."

"And?" Marcia asked Thomas, holding the cellphone to her ear. She was sitting up in bed with the TV on mute. The newscasters were reporting about President Johnson's son, Oscar, involved in a car accident in Florida. A dump truck traveling at top speed crashed into the vehicle he was riding in. He was in the hospital in critical condition. The driver of the dump truck was arrested and being investigated by the secret service.

Marcia was happy Thomas called; otherwise, she would have fallen asleep listening to the news. She had a bad habit of always watching the news to stay updated on the latest happenings, then fighting sadness based on what was reported.

"It's good. I'm at that part where it talks about, *What Can I Do?*"

"Okay. Let me get my book; we can read it together."

What Can I Do? *When God created you, He gave you a unique gift and talent. Have you ever thought of the things you are just naturally good at? Things that took little or no effort for you to do or understand? That right there could be a unique gift or talent. God gave that to you to use for His purpose and glory, to extend (support) the kingdom of God.*

The TV show American Idol is a contest to find the next great singer/performer. Many of the people trying out can't sing. They may think they sound great in the shower. I mean, who doesn't sound great singing in the shower? Unfortunately, it's not their natural gift. These contestants, who honestly cannot hold a note, are trying to do something they're not naturally gifted in. Then you hear the ones who are. It takes them little to no effort to hit the notes because it's their God-given unique gift.

Here are three ways to determine what you are called to do: 1. You will enjoy doing it. Whatever you're called to do (gifted in) will bring you joy in doing it. 2. When you discover what you're called to do, you will be good at it. Michael Jordan was a great basketball player but a subpar baseball player. He was naturally gifted in one and not the other. 3. When you find out what you're gifted in, you will have an opportunity to accomplish it. In Proverbs 18:16: it says that your gift will make room for you. Your gift will also be confirmed by others. When you specialize in something, it means you have become good at what you do, and this is unique for each person.

Marcia and Thomas discussed their opinions on the message for a few minutes. Marcia soon pushed the book aside, saying, "I miss you." She pouted. Their long-distance relationship was starting to take a toll on her emotionally. She constantly longed for his presence.

"I miss you, too. Bishop has an event in Las Vegas in a few days. I can buy you a ticket to come. We can hang out and sightsee on my downtime since you've never been to Vegas."

"It can only work if it's on the weekend. This Friday is a half-day, but if I give notice by tomorrow, I can get that day off. I can make arrangements for my neighbor Mrs. Crockett to watch the kids."

"We're getting into Vegas Friday morning. The event is the next day in the morning, then again Sunday morning for a couple of hours. Other than that, I will be free. Can you, maybe, see if you can also get Monday off so that you can fly back later that day?"

"I can do you one better. I will take Tuesday off, too, so I can come back that day. I'm due some personal days, and I really miss you."

Thomas smiled. "Great. I'll make arrangements and send you the details."

Marcia squealed. "I'm so excited! I've never been to the west coast."

"Awww, and here I thought your excitement was about getting to see me," he teased.

"That, too. I love you."

"I love you, too. You should probably go to sleep. I know it's past your bedtime."

Marcia yawned. She'd been stalling it for a while. "Yeah, I'm tired. But I wanted to wait up to talk to you."

"Thanks. I'm an hour behind you, remember. I at least have an hour more to kill before I hit the sack."

"Okay. Good night."

"Sweet dreams. I will call you tomorrow with the details."

***

Marcia was beside herself with excitement. She didn't even care that it was hot. As soon as she walked out of McCarran International Airport, the humidity welcomed her with a hug. But she kept a smile on her now sweaty face. Thomas was supposed to meet her at the airport. But when she landed and powered up her phone, there was a text from him saying he wouldn't arrive in Vegas until a little later. However, he arranged for a car service to pick her up.

Marcia saw her name on a sign held by a Hispanic woman in her mid-thirties dressed in a tuxedo skirt suit. The woman had a pleasant smile and didn't seem to be dying from the heat in her black outfit.

"Hi, I'm Marcia Jackson," she said to the driver.

"Welcome to Las Vegas, Ms. Jackson. I'm Veronica. I will be your driver. Please, let me assist you with your luggage." After shaking hands, Veronica took the handle of Marcia's carryon suitcase.

After arriving at the five-star hotel, Marcia went to the counter to check-in.

"Which room will you be staying in? Your name wasn't indicated either as a preference. One is larger than the other if that makes a difference," the clerk said.

"I'm okay with the smaller one." Marcia was thankful enough that Thomas bought her a ticket; she didn't want to come across as greedy in taking the larger room.

"Perfect. You're all checked in. Here is the keycard to your room."

Marcia checked into her room and freshened up before going downstairs to wait for Thomas at one of the hotel restaurants. His earlier text message said to meet him for lunch at twelve. She couldn't wait to see him. When they finish with lunch, Marcia wanted to walk the strip, and later, take a dip in the pool she'd noticed from her room's window.

"While you wait, would you like some water and bread?" the waiter asked.

"Yes, thank you."

Marcia picked up the menu. Upon opening it, she saw a message in bold, all caps: **WILL YOU MARRY ME?**

Shocked, she slapped the menu closed and looked around. She opened the menu again, reading the words. Tears pooled in her eyes. Loud applause stole her attention. She put down the menu, finding Thomas down on bended knee, holding the most beautiful and perfect ring.

"Marcia, I knew you were someone special from the moment I met you. I let fear stand in the way of pursuing you sooner, but I'm happy you finally agreed to date me. Now I'm taking a bolder step and asking you to be my wife. Will you do me the honor of being my wife? My queen? My one and only?"

Marcia nodded with happiness. She cupped his cheeks and said, "Yes!" She kissed him. "Yes!"

She kissed him again. "A million times, yes." Pulling back, she gazed into his eyes.

Thomas smiled. He was happy and relieved. He was a nervous wreck planning the engagement, unsure if she would say yes. He took her hand and slid the ring on her finger. People in the restaurant applauded. He stood.

Thomas helped her to her feet and hugged her. She spoke in the crook of his neck. "Are you really here for work?"

He laughed, shaking his head. "No. The kids and I have been planning this for a while."

Marcia pulled back in surprise. "What?"

Thomas helped her back in her seat, and sat across from her. "I asked Lisa, James, and Jada for your hand in marriage." He reached across the table and held her hand. He loved seeing his ring on her finger.

Tears pooled again. "Are they here, too?" She looked around.

"No. They wanted us to have our moment alone. They want us to throw a wedding party next weekend after we're married."

"Next weekend … after we're married …" She looked confused.

"I was hoping by this time tomorrow you would be my wife." Thomas' heart rate kicked up a notch again. She accepted his proposal, but would she be ready to make things official by tonight? They'd completed premarital counseling. He was working toward moving back to Maryland, and their kids approved of their relationship. All that was left was her being his wife.

"You want to get married now?" She needed clarity.

"Yes, if you don't think it's too soon."

"Let's do it! Let's get married."

"You have no idea how happy I am right now. I love you, Marcia. I love your children, too. I will be a great husband to you and stepdad to them. I will be the husband God needs me to be to you. I will love you like He loves the church. I want to spend the rest of my life loving you."

"Thank you for loving my children and me. I love you, and I love your son, too. I look forward to being a bonus mom to him. I will be a Proverbs 31 woman and wife to you. I want to spend the rest of my life loving you."

Holding hands, they looked into each other's eyes with tears. "You think we will remember that later in front of the minister?"

Marcia laughed, wiping tears. "Let's go find out."

Two hours later, they were officially husband and wife. Marcia wore a dress picked out by Lisa and Jada, an off-white designer mermaid style gown, which perfectly accentuated her figure. Thomas wore a tux he had tailored to fit him nicely. At the bridal suite, which was the larger of the two rooms he'd booked. He picked Marcia up bridal style, which caused her to giggle, before carrying her across the threshold of the room.

"Now it's official," Thomas joked with Marcia in his arms.

"Carrying me across the threshold made it official? Not the minister announcing us husband and wife?" She teased.

"It did. But after I get you out of this gorgeous gown, we will be making it official, *official*." He gently pressed his lips against hers, resulting in a passionate kiss.

"I like the sound of that," she replied against his lips.

Chapter 24

"And the LORD visited Sarah as he had said, and the LORD did unto Sarah as he had spoken. For Sarah conceived, and bare Abraham a son in his old age, at the set time of which God had spoken to him. And Abraham was a hundred years old when his son Isaac was born unto him. And Sarah said, God hath made me laugh so that all that hear will laugh with me. And she said, Who would have said unto Abraham, that Sarah should have given children suck? for I have born him a son in his old age." (Genesis 21:1-2,5-7)

Is there anything too hard for God? Whenever God makes us a promise, we can be sure it will come to pass. God isn't limited by our limitations. God told Abraham and Sarah they would have a child. Time didn't change that truth, though time did change Abraham and Sarah. What makes the miracle so amazing is the fact that Sarah conceived, carried the baby full term, and didn't die from childbirth at her old age without the aid of modern medicine. Also, Abraham was probably close to being impotent, especially when Viagra wasn't created yet. I had to throw that in there, so his ability to conceive a child was miraculous.

What thing has God promised you, and you feel too much time has passed with no chance for your prayer to be answered? It's declared today that it's not over! God is

faithful to what He said. In accordance with His will, He will answer your prayer.

Seven weeks passed, and married life was going along smoothly for Thomas and Marcia. He'd moved back to Maryland. His home there was larger, with a basement, than Marcia's house, so they decided on his place as their home together. Marcia placed her house for rent. She didn't want to get rid of it just yet. It was the home she and her deceased first husband had bought together. She and Thomas agreed it would be best, for now, to keep it for her kids' benefit.

Living together wasn't as awkward as they all had initially assumed it would be. For Marcia and Thomas, it felt like living with a best friend and lover. Jada and James loved Thomas as much as he loved them; they all had mutual respect for one another. Naturally, Jada rebelled at times, as a teenager would, when Thomas enforced rules, but she eventually obeyed. James and Jada liked having a man in the house because it took a lot of pressure off their mom. Because Thomas was a great stepdad, they were able to do things with him that they couldn't with their father. The fact that Thomas was white didn't matter at all.

Thomas was away for work in Miami. Marcia received a call from Jada's school saying she was sick with the stomach flu. Usually, when Thomas was home, he was able to get to the kids if she was at work or otherwise busy. Today, she left work early to pick up Jada and took her home to be taken care of.

Marcia got Jada settled in bed with a pail nearby for when she needed to throw up. Thankful the weather was warm enough, Marcia opened the windows in the house, allowing fresh air to flow through. She also sprayed Lysol in every room, hoping to kill the virus and prevent everyone else in the house from getting sick.

The next day, Marcia called in sick from work. When she rose that morning to check on Jada, Marcia made a quick beeline to the toilet to throw up. She didn't stop until her stomach was empty, and she was dry heaving.

Jada was back to normal health after 24 hours. It had now been three days, and Marcia was still throwing up. She was beginning to get worried because not only was she sick, but she hadn't received her period. Aunt Flo came on time every month. *Unless? God, please, don't let it be so!* Marcia thought in horror.

Weakly, she reached for her cellphone on the nightstand.

"Hey, babe, how are you feeling?" Thomas answered the call.

"I'm late."

He was confused. "Late, when are you coming home?"

"I am home; you're the one out of town."

"Right." He laughed. "Late for what then? I thought you were staying in bed today."

"Late as in my period. The only times I've been late were the three times I was pregnant."

Thomas was silent.

"Did you hear me, Thomas? I missed my period. I'm fifty. I cannot miss my period." She was beginning to get hysterical.

"Try to relax, babe. I will use one of the delivery apps and have a pregnancy test delivered to the house. Call me when it gets there so that we can see the results together. Whatever the results are, though, I want you to make an appointment to see the doctor."

"Okay. Have it delivered, and I will call you back."

Forty-five minutes later, Marcia was urinating on the pregnancy test stick. Thomas was on Facetime with the phone propped up on the vanity. After washing up, she anxiously paced, waiting for the timer taken from the kitchen to sound.

"I can't be pregnant, Thomas."

"If you are, it will be okay."

"You can't be serious. We're fifty! We have two kids in college and two in high school. I do not want to have any more kids. If we had gotten married ten years ago, I would be okay with it. But not now. I can't."

Thomas was torn. He wished he was there to console her. He wouldn't be able to until tomorrow afternoon when he flew back from work. "Marcia, we may be fifty, but we have many more healthy and prosperous years ahead of us. We can have a baby. A perfect blend of the two of us." He smiled.

"You just retired. Now you have this amazing position traveling as Bishop T. D. Forbes' head security man. I have ten years before I decide to retire. When Jada and James finish high school and go to college, we could use that time to travel and be kid-free. Not old parents to a baby, then toddler, then teen. We will be almost seventy by the time our baby graduates from high school."

"Please, don't get so worked up about this. We don't even know if you're pregnant."

The timer dinged. Marcia's heart was beating like a stampede in her chest.

"Check the results," Thomas coaxed her.

She nervously crept over to the bathroom counter. Seeing the lines almost caused her to faint. She gripped the vanity for support. "Thomas, you need to get home now!"

"What does it say."

"I'm pregnant!" she cried. Fat tears rolled into her mouth. "Oh, God! This can't be happening. After thirteen years of no sex, I get pregnant at fifty. You're the cause of this!"

"Why are you blaming me? You're the one always telling me not to stop." He chuckled.

Marcia groaned in agony.

"This is good news, Marcia. I'm happy you're pregnant. I love Lisa, James, and Jada, and I've always wanted another biological child. We're going to be fine. You're going to be fine. This is a blessing from the Lord."

Lying anxiously on the examination table in the doctor's office, Marcia understood there was going to be a need to seek counseling again from Dr. Lynn when her OB-GYN confirmed not only was she pregnant, she was carrying twins. Seeing the two peas in the pod on the screen and hearing their heartbeats was overwhelming.

Feeling overwhelmed with joy, Thomas leaned over and kissed Marcia on the forehead.

Marcia smiled weakly. She felt in her heart being pregnant at her age with twins, was a blessing. Getting her mind to agree was a different story.

Jada was happy when Marcia and Thomas broke the news to them. Lisa was on Facetime on Marcia's phone. Thomas' son, Karter, was on Facetime on his phone.

The other kids groaned. Marcia nodded, still trying to come to grips with her condition.

"Your mom is seven weeks pregnant with twins."

The four siblings' mouths hung open. "Wow, congratulations," they all said in their own way. They were shocked but happy about the news.

"Dad and Marcia, I'm happy for you guys," Karter said with a smile. "Marcia, Lisa, James, and Jada I love the way you all make me feel like part of the family. Even though I'm on the west coast, I get a call from all of you every week. I can't wait to move back to D.C. after I graduate to start my job with the government and be close to family. Those twins you're having are going to be greatly loved."

Marcia wiped tears. "Thank you, Karter. I love you!"

"I love you, too, Marcia."

"Welcome to the new chapter of our lives, guys. The twins will be here in a few months."

Chapter 25

"First of all, then, I urge that supplications, prayers, intercessions, and thanksgivings be made for all people, 2 for kings and all who are in high positions, that we may lead a peaceful and quiet life, godly and dignified in every way." (1 Timothy 2:1-2)

Regardless of our political affiliations, it is important to pray for our president and government officials. Because of the complex and dangerous challenges of running a nation, as Christians, we must ask God for wisdom and protection for our leaders. We should pray that our leaders walk in godly integrity, that they may be accountable to the people and not their selfish desires. And that our leaders be surrounded by godly counsel. If we are Christians, this is something we are mandated to do – pray, regardless of who is in office.

In the Scripture above, Paul instructed Timothy to pray for the rulers of their day. When the Roman Empire was persecuting the church and feeding them to the lions, Paul knew despite the persecution that prayer would be the avenue God would use to change the hearts of the leaders. When President Obama was president, there was racial divide with having the first black president of the United States, among other things. Today, with President Trump in office, there is still division over some of his policies.

Regardless of whether we were pro Obama or pro-Trump – if they fail, we fail as an American nation. But we can all win if we pray for whoever is in office.

As Christians, we are called to a higher standard. As believers, we must live a godly life. Our behavior should remain the same whether we're on the job or in our cars driving in rush hour traffic. We shouldn't result to using offensive words or putting up our middle fingers. We shouldn't gossip or steal pens and paper from work. We are the light of the world. Light is something that gives a clear vision.

We must live a life that reflects the heart of our King. In the gospel of Mark 12:17, Jesus never spoke ill of Caesar, the first Roman Emperor, He respected the rules of His day. Then Jesus said to them, "Pay to Caesar the things that belong to Caesar. Pay to God the things that belong to God." They were surprised and wondered at Him.

During one of her therapy sessions, Dr. Lynn told Marcia that Brent Nelson, the author of the book she'd read, *Journey to Faith*, was recently voted in as pastor of a church in Alexandria, Virginia. The church had about 150 members.

Marcia was excited. She wanted to meet him. She'd shared the book with so many people. It was a book she picked up often to read, especially now that she was struggling with being fifty and pregnant with twins. She was now three months pregnant and was starting to show with a slight baby bump. At her age, plus carrying multiples, Marcia was considered high risk. So far, all tests had checked out fine, and she was forever grateful to God for perfect health. She was also coming to terms with her new reality. Therapy was helping. *Our plans aren't always God's plans.*

Getting to Jesus is Lord church thirty minutes before the service, Thomas and Marcia found seats in the second room. They gleaned every word from Pastor Nelson as he preached a word about faith.

Pastor Nelson, an average height black man in his late forties, addressed the congregation, then went into his message. "I'm teaching from Hebrews 11:1. In this Scripture, every time you see the word faith, I want you to replace it with the word trust. Because we may often use faith as a tool to get what we want from God, but trust is a better approach to understanding the heart and mind of God. Sometimes what we want may not be good for us, and we think faith is a blank check we can use whenever we want something. I want my children to ask me for things, however I want them to trust my motive, intention, and timing. Faith requires not just to believe God, but to trust Him also.

If you can, I want you to jot down these acronyms I have for faith; they will also be posted on the screens:

T – **Trust** always requires a test. I saw a guy shadowboxing one day while I was at a red light. He looked tough, but there was no real challenge to determine this because he was only fighting the air. Trusting in God requires a test of our faith, that we believe Him in spite of what we see. The Bible teaches that without faith, it is impossible to please God.

R – True trust requires a **relationship** with God. Imagine if our kids would only ask us for things and don't want to spend time with us or get our opinion on things? It is important to spend time in prayer and meditation with God to build a relationship.

U – Trust in God is like an **umbrella**. It doesn't stop the rain but provides covering. God doesn't stop the storms of life, but He provides shelter from them. Trust doesn't mean we are immune to trouble, but in our troubles, God is with us.

S – We need to **surrender** to God's will and way. We have to say, 'Not my will, but Your will be done.' Surrender means to be a living sacrifice to the one who has created us. We must submit our will under God's will.

T – We must become **teachable** in what God is telling us to do. When babies are learning how to walk, falling doesn't matter as long as they get back up and try again. Parents have their hands outstretched in encouragement. God has His hands outstretched, encouraging us to continue on our journey of faith.

As I close, trust means we don't have to know all the answers, but we're putting our trust and faith in someone who does. He is the author and finisher of our faith."

At the end of his teaching, Pastor Nelson asked Deacon Lee to pray for the people of the church, the nation with all the tragedies occurring, and those affected in the Bahamas from hurricane Dorian. He also asked Deacon Lee to pray for the president.

Pastor Nelson passed the microphone over to Deacon Lee, and he began praying. "Lord, we ask You to bless the church. We pray the church, as a whole, would be a place of refuge for the hurting and the lost. We pray all the people affected by the tragedies in our nation and world would not become bitter and help them to forgive those who have inflicted pain. We pray for the Bahamas and all those affected. I also want to thank the church and everyone who donated items and gave monetary donations that were given to the Bahamas Embassy as part of the relief efforts. I pray for healing for them, emotionally, mentally, and physically, and that they will rebuild better than they were before.

I pray they will seek Your face, Father. Continue to guide and protect us, Lord. I pray for the man in the white house—I mean the president. I pray the Lord will continue to break him and strip him to nothing. You're already bringing him to his knees, Lord, with his daughter Ava being sick and his son Oscar still recovering from the car accident.

There's a saying my grandmother used, 'the chicken has come home to roost,' which means bad things that someone has done in the past have come back to bite them. Lord, You said a man would reap what he sowed. He wants to make America great again, huh?"

Pastor Nelson stopped him. "No. No! Please stop!"

The congregation was in shock. Thomas and Marcia were uncomfortable with where the prayer was going.

"According to the Bible, we are told to pray for our president, not curse and mock him." Pastor Nelson continued. "How can you justify praying to God to strip a man and bring him to his knees? He's a father — a husband. And, most importantly, the president of the United States. Go back and read 1 Timothy 2:1-2. What you were doing wasn't praying. It was a blatant display of hatred and maybe even racism on your part. Even if the president is wrong in some of his policies and procedures, how can two wrongs make a right? We are Christians and should be the light of the world. We shouldn't lower our standards because of the God we serve."

Deacon Lee looked angry and embarrassed. He dropped the microphone and walked off the stage. Pastor Nelson noticed Minister Myra Hannah went after him.

Despite the awkward prayer at the end, the service was amazing. Thomas and Marcia waited in line to speak to Pastor Nelson and have him sign their books.

As they waited their turn, Thomas periodically placed his hand on Marcia's small bump. She smiled up at him. He took the opportunity to kiss her on the forehead. "I can't wait until we can feel them moving."

"I can," she said. "It's two of them in there. I don't look forward to them kickboxing on my bladder."

"Oh, yeah. That probably won't be fun."

She shook her head. "Nope, but maybe they will have mercy on me."

"I'll talk with them to take it easy on their mama."

Soon it was their turn.

"The service was amazing," Marcia said, shaking Pastor Nelson's hand. "I was introduced to your book over a year ago. I've been telling so many people about it. When I found out you were coming to Maryland, I had to come and meet you."

Pastor Nelson smiled. "Thank you. I appreciate you coming out."

"I liked how you handled the situation with the deacon," Thomas said.

"Do you understand why I interrupted him?"

"We did. We were getting uncomfortable with it and wondered when someone was going to put a stop to it," Thomas answered.

"For God to promote us, we must respect His word. His word is clear that we are called to bless and not hurt. It's hard to pray for someone and criticize them at the same time. In the Bible, David was loyal to Saul, his king, even though Saul tried to kill him. David respected the office of the king even though the man didn't act the way he should have. How much more should we respect the office of the president?"

"I agree. And despite the things I don't agree with President Johnson, I do sympathize with him regarding his daughter being sick and his son recovering from an accident. On top of that, he's being investigated by the Department of Justice while being commander and chief of such a great nation. He's under a lot of pressure."

"Indeed, he is, which is why we need to pray." Pastor said, accepting the copies of their books they wanted autographed.

"My wife introduced me to your book a few months back, and I gave a copy of it to Bishop Forbes. He loves it."

"Wow, really? That's amazing. I'm honored. I would love to meet him one day."

"I work for him. Maybe I can see what I can do. Bishop has an event in D.C. in a few weeks."

"At the Way of Jesus Church?" Pastor Nelson asked.

"Yes. You've heard of the event?"

"Absolutely. I'm not on the panel, but I'd planned to be there."

"Perfect. Maybe I can arrange for you two to meet."

Pastor Nelson was grateful. "Thank you. I would greatly appreciate the opportunity." He gave them back their signed books.

"You're welcome. I can't make any promises because Bishop is busy. But I have a feeling he will be able to fit you in. Give me your contact info, and I will keep in touch."

Thomas and Pastor Nelson pulled out their phones and exchanged numbers.

"It was great meeting you. We plan to visit your church again." Marcia chimed in, walking away for the next person in line.

Later, Pastor Nelson meet with Deacon Lee in his office, along with Minister Myra Hannah.

Pastor Nelson addressed the deacon, "Deacon Lee, I want to thank you for everything you've done for us at the church thus far. When I was voted into this church, you were supportive of my family and me. I know we couldn't have made it without you. Right now, I need you to explain to me what motivated you to say the things you did about our president during prayer?"

Deacon Lee answered defensively. "I still don't see what I said as wrong. When Obama was president, the Republicans and white folks talked about him like he was a dog. They didn't even believe he was born in America. Now we have Johnson following in forty-five's footsteps. The Bible says whatever a man sows, he will reap." Deacon sat up straighter, leaning forward indignantly. "And, young man, you don't want to get on my bad side. You already embarrassed me out there in front of everyone. Just remember the same way you were voted in, you can be voted out!"

Minister Hannah interjected, "Deacon Lee, do you think it was fair talking about the man's children like that? Ava has cancer, and Oscar is still recovering in the hospital from the car accident. Hatred and racism are wrong regardless of who is projecting it. We are not a hate group; we are a church."

"Ha," Deacon Lee laughed dryly at Myra. "You're lucky you're even sitting here. Minister Hannah. I'm not used to women ministers; it was only because of him," he pointed a finger to Pastor Nelson. "That women were allowed in ministry here. I don't care about them other churches with women pastors and such. Don't think you, him, and the rest of the couple of females in ministry won't get voted out, too!"

"Deacon Lee, you will publicly denounce what you said and apologize for the hatred and bitterness you expressed from the pulpit that is anti-Christian. And I'm going to sit you down for six weeks as a disciplinary action. Then you will be placed on probation for one year. If anything like this happens again, you will be removed from your position."

Deacon Lee stood. "What the hell? I will do no such thing! And you're not taking away my position. I brought you here, and I can take you out. One of us won't be here in six weeks and take a guess on which one of us that will be." He flipped the chair and stormed out of the office.

Chapter 26

"Do not despise this small beginning, for the eyes of the Lord rejoice to see the work begin, to see the plumb line in the hand of Zerubbabel. For these seven lamps represent the eyes of the Lord that see everywhere around the world." (Zechariah 4:10)

Sometimes when God is going to do a great work, He may start with something small. Microscopic – so small as to be visible only with a microscope. When I was in the seventh grade, my science teacher shared a story. While he was on vacation in Mexico, with his wife and two daughters, he told them not to drink the water because of the parasites in the water. Parasites aren't easily visible through the naked eye. Soon his daughters became sick with diarrhea, nausea, vomiting, and fevers. He asked them if they drank the water. They told him no; they only had ice. My science teacher asked the class, "Why did my daughters get sick?

One of my classmates raised a hand, answering, "Because ice and water are the same things, they just have a different form. The parasites were in the water as well as the ice."

My teacher replied, "You answered correctly."

Your success today may be microscopic right now – unseen by the naked eye. But if you trust the process of seed time and harvest, you will see the greatness of the seed. A seed, while growing, will change from one stage to another. Every stage is important for proper growth. To be successful, you must sow a good seed to reap a harvest. Malcolm Gladwell has something called the 10,000-Hour Rule. It is twenty hours a week for ten years. This is needed to become world-class in any field. For instance, Serena Williams started playing tennis at the age of six, and at the age of seventeen, she won her first Grand Slam. She couldn't have succeeded if she hadn't practiced her serve, volley, backhand, and conditioning. It takes sacrifice to succeed in anything, and that sacrifice is the seed to success. Seed and success are synonymous like ice and water.

Our success may be microscopic now, but we must not become weary while we're waiting on the Lord.

Early the next morning, while at the drive-thru, placing an order for coffee and breakfast, Pastor Nelson received a call from Minister Hannah.

"Good morning, Myra," he answered after paying for his order.

"Get to the church now!" She shouted.

"I'm on my way; I just stopped for breakfast. What's going on?"

"Deacon Lee called an emergency board meeting."

Nelson internally groaned. The deacon and his antics were starting to give him a headache. "I'm on my way." He received his order and thanked the person at the drive-thru window.

A few minutes later, he pulled into the church and noticed his reserved parking space was occupied with another car, Deacon Lee's. Nelson bit his tongue and found another spot to park in. Forgetting his coffee and breakfast, he made his way into the church. Loud voices coming from one of the meeting rooms told him where everyone was.

Minister Hannah noticed him before he stepped into the room. She met him at the door. "They're trying to vote you out. Can they do that? You've only been here a few months."

"They're the board; they can do what they want. I would hope they don't, though." He stepped further into the room. All heads turned toward him.

"Aww, your little birdie told you we were meeting today?" Deacon Lee mocked. "Well, have a seat, so you're front and center when we vote your hind out of this church."

The twelve-person board, a mixture of men and women, murmured. Everyone took their seats. Since she wasn't part of the board, Myra stood near the door.

"Everyone is aware of what happened yesterday. Being head of this board, I called this emergency meeting to vote whether or not we should keep you on. Anything you'd like to say before we vote, Mr. Nelson?"

"It's still Pastor Nelson. And yes, I have something to say. I stand by my calling you out yesterday. As Christians, we are called to a higher standard. And what you did, Deacon Lee, praying in front of the congregation, mocking the president was ungodly. And if you all feel what he did was right and my response was wrong, so be it. I've enjoyed being the pastor of this church and working with all of you. I had great vision for advancement for the congregation and programs to help the community as well. I would hate to leave, but either way, I know the Lord will provide."

"Now that he's done," Deacon Lee said, sneering at Nelson. "Let's vote. All in favor of *not* keeping Brent Nelson as pastor of the church, raise your hand."

All twelve members raised their hands without any hesitation. Nelson was hurt. He shook his head in disbelief. He'd only been there for a few months but thought he had formed great relationships with all members of the board. He was also well-loved and received by the congregation. When he came on, the church barely had 100 members, and now it was 150. He was bringing growth. Now because he took a stand against a wrong, he was ousted.

Nelson bowed his head and silently prayed. He got up and quietly left the room. Minister Hannah followed.

Like Nelson, his wife and children were disappointed about the news. They vowed to get through it together as a family. Nelson devoted himself to a time to fast and pray about the situation. *Do not despise the day of small beginnings,* he kept hearing in his spirit.

Even though Nelson didn't have a church, the calling to teach was still on his life. A couple of days later, while writing a sermon in his home office, he received a call from a buddy, Clayton Smith.

"What's up, Clayton?"

"I'm good. I've got some interesting news for you."

"Yeah? What's that?"

"The board members at my church, House of Worship, in Fort Washington, are looking for a senior pastor because the recent one abruptly accepted a new position out of state. I mentioned you, and with your resume and experience, I think you're a shoo-in. We're a nondenominational church. Seventy-five members. I know it's small, but with you, we can do big things."

Nelson almost dropped his cellphone. He leaned back in his desk chair, marveling at the news. *God, is this what you have for me?*

"The board would like to meet with you tomorrow. They're anxious to have someone nominated to preach on Sunday."

Sunday was three days away.

"I have to talk with my wife. I can let you know something later today."

"Awesome. Thanks! This will be a great position for you, Brent. I know it."

"Thanks, Clayton. I will let you know something soon."

That Sunday morning, Pastor Brent Nelson was introduced as the new senior pastor at House of Worship Church.

***

Thomas was shocked that Bishop Forbes agreed to meet with Pastor Nelson. He was a personable man and great to be around, but he was the bishop, which meant he stayed busy. For him to set aside thirty minutes to meet with Pastor Nelson was amazing. Since being on staff, many people asked Thomas for favors by setting up meetings with the bishop. He always declined. For some reason, he promised Pastor Nelson he would set a meeting up.

"Hi, Thomas," Nelson said, after answering the call.

It had been eight days since they'd met.

"I guess you saved my number."

"I did."

"I'm calling to let you know Bishop has agreed to meet with you when he's in town. It will have to be at the event. He has thirty minutes to spare right before the event starts. I will email you the details."

Nelson fist-pumped the air. *God, You are amazing. All of this in a week.* "Thank you, Thomas. A meeting like this is maybe once in a lifetime. I can't thank you enough."

"No thanks needed. My wife and I thoroughly enjoyed your book. And like I said, Bishop read and enjoyed it, too. He's honored to meet you as well."

"I appreciate it."

"My wife and I decided we want to join your church. We plan on bringing the kids with us on Sunday."

Nelson cleared his throat. "Actually, after that prayer situation the Sunday you and your wife attended, I was voted out of the church by the deacon and the board. But the Lord blessed me with a new congregation a few days later. I'm now the senior pastor at House of Worship Church in Fort Washington, Maryland. I hope that's not too far for you. My family and I would love for you to become members there."

"I will speak with Marcia, but I don't think that would be a problem. It's not far from us at all."

Chapter 27

"When someone becomes a Christian, he becomes a brand-new person inside. He is not the same anymore. A new life has begun!" (2 Corinthians 5:17)

Are you a prisoner of shame? Are you a prisoner of your past? People sometimes love to remind us of our past and who we used to be. They say that a zebra can't change its stripes. This may be true for the zebra, but we aren't zebras, we are made in the image of God. God can change our hearts and minds, which will lead to a change in our actions and behaviors.

The late Billy Graham once told a story titled "Under New Management." He said while preaching and traveling, he went to a restaurant near his motel. There wasn't a hostess available, so he seated himself. He waited for almost fifteen minutes before a waitress came to take his order. "Good morning, sir. We don't have coffee, eggs, toast, bacon, sausage, ham, orange juice, grits, steak..."

Graham asked, "What do you have?"

She replied, "We have cereal, but we don't have milk?" She also stated they had donuts, which he ordered.

When Graham went to the restroom, he noticed there wasn't soap to wash his hands. When he got back to the table, roaches were crawling on it. Graham got his donuts and left. This motel was in a remote area, and the only place he could eat and sleep within a fifty-mile radius. The following year, Graham returned to the area and went back to the restaurant to eat. As he walked in, he was pleasantly greeted by a hostess and escorted to a table. Moments later, a waitress greeted him with a smile to take his order. Graham asked, "What are you out of?"

The waitress was surprised by the question. "We're not out of anything, sir."

Graham asked, "You have coffee?"

She replied, "Yes, bacon, toast, steak..." On and on, he asked, and she replied yes.

He went to the bathroom and found it clean with plenty of soap. When he returned to the table, there were no roaches, his food was hot, and waiting. The waitresses asked, "You're not from around these parts, are you?'

He said, "No, I came here a year ago. This place was totally different than what it is now."

She said, "You didn't see the sign that we are under new management?"

It's important to understand we can change our circumstances if we change our minds and manage our lives differently. When we fully allow God into our lives, we are also "under new management."

Nelson still couldn't believe he was sitting across from Bishop T. D. Forbes. He recalled his fourteen-year-old daughter, Judea, from being a baby up until around two years old. She could be crying or playing, but whenever she heard Bishop's voice on TV she stopped whatever she was doing to listen to him speak.

"It's an honor to meet with you," Nelson told Bishop. They were in a room filled with a few people. As the minister prepped to go on stage for the event, people were attaching his microphone, applying stage makeup, and making sure his clothes were in order.

"Thomas gave me a copy of your book a while ago, and I've been reading pages whenever I get a chance. It's good! I'm sure many people will be blessed from reading it like I have."

"I appreciate the encouragement. You know how it is when God tells you to do something, you must do it. He kept bringing it up in my mind until I had no choice but to obey."

Bishop laughed heartedly. "Yes, I know. I'm just hurt you didn't ask me to write your foreword."

"Trust me; if I knew how to reach you and that you would've done it, I would've. You can still write me a review."

"I got you. I'm happy you obeyed God because I want to give a copy of your book to the president. I'm meeting with him soon."

Nelson's eyes grew wide like saucers. This was beyond his wildest imagination. He was at a lost for words. "I ... wow ... that would be great."

"How would you like to be the one to give it to the president yourself?"

The president may not have been the most favorable right now. Nelson still felt to have him read *Journey to Faith* would be an honor. It was written to help draw people closer to God.

"When and where, and I will be there."

"On stage in ten!" Someone called out.

Bishop rose. "I will have my assistant send the details." He held out his hand to Nelson for a handshake. "It was nice meeting you. Stay encouraged. I have a feeling God has big plans coming right around the corner for you. Get ready!"

Nelson had never been to the White House, and it would be a day he wouldn't soon forget. He wore one of his best suits. A black Armani suit with a white dress shirt and blue tie. He got a tapered haircut, to his salt and pepper hair, yesterday. He was looking debonair. He said a silent prayer, asking God for wisdom.

"I see you are looking sharp," Thomas greeted Nelson.

Nelson had just made it through security to get into the white house. Bishop T. D. Forbes and his team were already inside.

Nelson and Thomas gave each other a bro hug. "Thanks, man. I'm not late, am I?"

"No. You both will be escorted by the secret service to meet the president in twenty minutes."

"Cool." Nelson took in the grandeur of being in the white house. He was almost afraid to touch anything. In a way it felt like he was in a museum.

Soon, he and Bishop greeted each other and chatted as they waited. Then they were escorted to the Treaty Room for their private meeting with the president. Nelson wished it was the Oval Office so that he could take a picture. But his cellphone was confiscated.

Bishop and Nelson received warm greetings from President Johnson. He was an average height, white man in his late sixties with salt and pepper hair. He was dressed in a dark suit minus the jacket. Nelson thought he would feel a sense of arrogance from President Johnson, surprisingly there wasn't.

"Thank you, gentlemen, for meeting with me," President Johnson said, taking a seat.

Bishop pleasantly replied.

"It's a pleasure to meet you, Mr. President. I brought a copy of my book, *Journey to Faith,* for you." Nelson stood, handing the book to the president.

"Thank you, Pastor Nelson. In preparation for you attending this meeting with Bishop Forbes, I was told about your book and got a copy. I've been reading it. It's been an eyeopener, especially with all the personal things I'm dealing with. I'm sure you're aware."

Nelson nodded.

"Yes, we're aware," Bishop answered. "I'm happy you reached out for Christian counsel."

"Aside from the political issues I have, and the investigation, Ava is getting treatment for cancer; Oscar is now getting physical therapy to help him walk better again. All of this has put a strain on my marriage. My marriage wasn't perfect before I became president, but things have gotten worse." Johnson shook his head in thought. "As the president and businessman, I am used to making deals.

Successful deals! But I can't seem to make one with God."

"The most successful deal you can make with God is surrendering your life to him. Accept him as your Lord and personal Savior," Bishop Forbes said.

"Hmmm. Pastor Nelson, is that similar to accepting a friend request from God? You mentioned it in your book."

Nelson nodded. "Yes, it is. It's also in the Bible; Romans 10:9-10: 'If you say with your mouth that Jesus is Lord, and believe in your heart that God raised Him from the dead, you will be saved from the punishment of sin. When we believe in our hearts, we are made right with God. We tell with our mouth how we were saved from the punishment of sin.'"

"Simple as that?" Johnson asked.

"Yes. It's quite simple. Like Pastor Nelson mentioned in his book, God wants us to accept his friend request. However, he's not going to force us to. He wants us to accept Him, love Him, and in return, we receive forgiveness for our sins. And if we truly allow our friendship with God to influence our lives, we begin to become better people. Our old selves are no more," Bishop Forbes said.

"With the recent tragedies in my life, for the first time, I'm truly convinced there's someone bigger than I am." Johnson chuckled. "I'm the president of maybe the most powerful country in the world, yet my position couldn't prevent my daughter from getting leukemia or my son from almost getting killed in a car accident. My wife barely says two words to me unless we're in front of a camera." Johnson sighed deeply. "My lawyers have told me the special counsel will indict me because of the money I received from North Korea."

Bishop Forbes and Nelson looked at the president in surprise at his admission but remained quiet.

"I could fight this by invoking my executive privilege, but I'm just tired of fighting. The vice president assured me that when I resign, he will pardon me. I have made a mess of my life. I've hurt a lot of people. I've been a racist. I want to surrender to someone bigger than all this." He outstretched his arms in emphasis.

"God is the maker of the heavens and earth. The alpha and omega. There's no one greater than

Him. No other god compares. Surrender to him." Nelson urged the president.

The president asked, "Can God forgive me for all my sins?"

Bishop smiled with compassion and said, "Yes, He can. The word salvation comes from the word salvage, meaning to preserve someone or something from potential loss or adverse circumstances."

"Good because I have some adverse circumstances." The room grew quiet. "I want to accept God's friend request," the president informed them.

"Okay, let us pray with you, and you can accept Christ," Nelson said, standing.

Bishop stood as well. The president joined them at the center of the room. The men placed their hands on either shoulder of the president. Bishop began praying. "Repeat after me: Father, I come to You in the name of Jesus. I accept Jesus as my Lord and Savior. I believe you raised Jesus from the dead. I accept Jesus' righteousness in exchange for my sins."

Tears ran from the president's eyes. "Amen! Thank you, Jesus."

"Welcome to the family of God," Nelson said with a smile.

There was a knock on the door, indicating their meeting was to come to a close.

Nelson looked at Johnson. "Mr. President, in my book, today, if possible, I want you to read the section about: Who Am I? Where Am I From? Why Am I Here? What Can I Do? Where Am I Going?"

Johnson shook Nelson's hand. "Okay, I will. Thank you." He turned to Bishop. "Always a pleasure. I appreciate your counsel. You'll be hearing from me again soon."

Later, President Johnson read:

Where Am I Going? *If you don't know where you're going, you are considered lost. In life, it is essential to know where you're going to end up when your life is over. Faith tells you where you came from and where you are going. When you are born again, you receive a spiritual social security number that grants you access to heaven. If you wanted to come into the United States, you need proper documentation to be granted access. When you die, you want to have access to heaven or the kingdom of God. In Luke 10:20, Jesus said to rejoice that your* names are written in heaven. Our final destination in this life is access into the kingdom of God. By simply accepting Jesus Christ as your Lord and personal Savior, or accepting God's friend request, you will receive your spiritual social security number to heaven. The good news is you have been preapproved through Christ; your race doesn't matter, economic status doesn't matter, who your parents are doesn't matter, what you did in the past doesn't matter. Jesus said in John 14:3: "And if I go and prepare a place for you, I will come again, and receive you unto myself; that where I am, there ye may be also."

Chapter 28

"You will keep in perfect peace all who trust in you, all whose thoughts are fixed on you!" (Isaiah 26:3)

July 16, 1999, John F, Kennedy Jr., died with his wife Carolyn and her sister Lauren in a plane crash. The investigators concluded that John Jr. may have been confused about the position of his plane. He didn't know if his plane was turned up or down as it crashed into the ocean. This is called spatial disorientation. Spatial disorientation is the inability of a person to correctly determine his/her body position or location.

John Jr. was most likely looking out of his windshield rather than looking at his cockpit instruments. If it's perfect weather during the day, looking through the windshield while flying to determine direction is okay. However, during a storm or hazy weather, looking through the windshield to determine direction will be difficult. This is why knowing how to read the cockpit instruments are important.

The weather condition when he died was hazy; he should have had a more experienced pilot with him. In addition to the weather and his inexperience, his foot was in a cast, which made it hard to control the plane. Kennedy had not received his instrument rating that gives the pilot the ability to control and navigate an airplane by reference to the flight and navigation instruments. He was only certified to fly during visible conditions.

God has given man five senses: the ability to hear, smell, taste, feel, and see. I believe that faith/trust is a sixth sense every believer has and is a bridge between the spiritual and the natural. I believe faith is practical, as well as spiritual. We define faith as having confidence in someone or something. When the storms of life happen, we must first look to the one who created us and remember He is the author and finisher of our faith. Our circumstances are subject to change because of who He is. Kennedy might not have crashed his plane had he been trained in instrument flying.

It is easy to look at other things, and other people, when we are faced with heartache and pain, or be led by our senses. In a storm of life, our ability to see, hear, taste, feel, or smell can be compromised. Our senses can sometimes deceive us. Before the days of GPS, sailors used compasses or the stars to navigate the seas. The Bible tells us in Psalm 19:1: that the heavens declare the glory of God. If we can trust the moon, the sun, and the stars, how much more can we trust the one who created those things? This is why we are told to walk by faith, trust in God, and not be led by our senses.

Thomas and Marcia were enjoying a lazy day at home without the kids. Now that she was six months pregnant, the doctor recommended she cut back on hours at work. Marcia was doing well at her age and stage in pregnancy, but with the stress of working in a public school and some false alarms to the emergency room with issues with preeclampsia, made the decision necessary.

Thomas also urged Marcia to cut back. He was still working and receiving retirement income from the police department. Marcia agreed and reduced her work hours to three days a week. They were doing well financially. Together, they decided she would stay home with the twins after they were born.

They found out the sex of the babies a week ago. They were having a boy and a girl. Thomas couldn't be happier and couldn't wait to see their identical twins. Marcia had finally come to terms with the pregnancy and was also excited to be carrying mini versions of Thomas and herself. The family were all deciding on the best names for the babies and would vote soon. Their son's name would begin with a T, and their daughter's name would begin with an M.

The couple was cozy in their bed. Marcia was watching the news, and Thomas was reading a mystery novel.

Running across the bottom of the TV screen: *Breaking News: President tweets: We will never forget 9-11-01.*

The news host, Jimmy Black, spoke, "It's hard to imagine that it has been eighteen years since the terrorist attacks on America. Do you remember where you were when you heard about the attacks?"

The guest, Kishma Cartwright, answered, "It is hard to believe it's been eighteen years, Jimmy. It is a day I won't forget. Ever. It was a Tuesday, and I was on a train traveling back from Boston after a conference the day before. It was chaotic! All trains were halted, causing concern from all the passengers. Then people were receiving calls from friends and family members telling them what happened. People began to panic. I was trying to get back home to D.C. All car rentals were booked with people renting them to drive to their destinations. I happened to see a lady with D.C. tags, flagged her down, and asked her if I could hike a ride back to the city with her."

Jimmy nodded. "Yes, the country was in complete chaos. No one knew where the terrorists would strike next." Jimmy adjusted his earpiece as if listening intently to whoever was speaking in his ear.

Flashing boldly on the bottom of the screen: BREAKING NEWS!

Jimmy sat up straighter, displaying a shocked look. "We just got new breaking news. At exactly 10 a.m., there were ten violent incidents reported seemly simultaneously around the country. These attacks occurred in Delray Beach, Florida, near the Pentagon, in the D.C. area, Virginia, Seattle, Washington, New York, South Carolina, Ohio, and in Maryland."

Thomas and Marcia sat up with alarm. Marcia grabbed the remote and turned up the volume. "Oh, my goodness. Did you hear that?"

Thomas nodded.

"I repeat, at 10 a.m., there were ten simultaneous incidents all around the country. Could this be foreign terrorism? Domestic terrorism? We don't know. All we know is there is chaos; there is fear, and there is panic. Terror has taken a new name. And all of this on the anniversary of 9-11. It has just been announced that all emergency service workers, policemen, military, and firemen around the country have been put on mandatory duty until further notice."

BREAKING NEWS! BREAKING NEWS! BREAKING NEWS! BREAKING NEWS!

Jimmy was handed a piece of paper. "These are the areas that have been attacked.1. Shooting at a post office near the World Trade Center in New York; 2. Shooting at post office near the Pentagon in Arlington, Virginia; 3. Guards shot at the Department of Homeland Security office in Washington, D.C.; 4. Shooting at a government building in New York; 5. A man drove a car into a group of Hispanics in front of a hardware store in Seattle, Washington; 6. A man drove a car into a group of Hispanics in front of a hardware store in Delray Beach, Florida; 7. A gunman opened fire on a Jewish community congregation in Ohio; 8. Active shooter at a Walmart in Virginia; 9. Active shooter at a Jewish synagogue in Silver Spring, Maryland; and 10. Active shooter at Lovell University, a Historically Black College in South Carolina."

Marcia closed her eyes, and said, "Father God, I pray for your guidance and protection for all those involved. And I pray for the families of the lives that may have been lost. I rebuke the attacks. I pray the attackers will turn from their evil ways now, so no one else is hurt." Opening her eyes, Marcia reached over and gripped Thomas' hand. "What kind of world are we about to bring our babies into?"

"A fallen world, no doubt. We must rely on our faith to keep and protect our family and us." He lovingly placed his free hand on her protruding midsection. "The evil people doing this will have to also answer to God one day."

They grew quiet, staring at the report on the television.

Jimmy continued. "So far, multiple people have been reported dead in this planned attack, especially on the anniversary of our first major attack on America. This is evil, a blatant evil act. I hope all those involved are caught alive. The country, once again, is in a state of panic."

Marcia picked up her cellphone and called Lisa in Atlanta. Thomas got his phone and called Karter in California. Next, they were calling the school to have Jada and James released early. They needed to make sure their kids were safe.

Jesus protect America! Thomas prayed, hoping he wouldn't allow fear to overcome him.

Chapter 29

"And he will turn the hearts of the fathers to their children, and the hearts of the children to their fathers. Or else I will come and destroy the land with a curse." (Malachi 4:6)

What do you think are the greatest consequences of a fatherless generation? Homes without fathers may likely belong to the poor, and children may likely get involved in negative situations: drugs, alcohol, gangs, rebellion, the list is endless. Fatherless children may suffer from emotional problems. Boys are at a higher risk of criminal activity, and girls may likely become pregnant at an early age.

Too many young men and women are abandoned by either their mother or father, but too often, it's by their fathers, leaving their children to fend for themselves in a world without a mentor, protector, and provider. This can create a cycle of destruction that can pass on to generations. The side effects are seen in our society, where young people are mentoring each other, the blind leading the blind.

This issue isn't so much the absence of fathers, rather the absence of fatherhood, as stated in an article by Kris Vallotton. About 70 percent of African American women are unwed mothers, 50 percent of Hispanic women are unwed mothers, and 40 percent of Americans are unwed mothers.

I don't know anything about my biological father. I've never even seen a picture of him. This created a void and uncertainty in my life I never understood. There were many symptoms to the source of my problems I didn't understand needing approval, needing to define my identity. When becoming part of God's family, we identify Him as father. Though it doesn't erase the past, God is compensating for what we lost. I think it's sad that society, as a whole, has accepted the term "baby daddy."

The child support system is necessary, but like any system, it can be manipulated and unfair. If a man's license is taken or his credit is damaged, he isn't able to properly pay for living expenses. How can we fix this problem? I believe abortion is wrong. But what do we do with the children who are here and suffering?

In the same way that we are aggressive about a woman not aborting her child, we must also be aggressive in giving her the tools to maintain the longevity and health of the child after birth. We don't have to be biological fathers to be a father. Almost forty years ago, God blessed me with a stepfather that is still active in my life. Any man can create a child, but it takes a father to raise one. Our children need godly mentors with pure motives and accountability.

Vallotton, K. (2019, January 30). 5 Concerning Cultural Side Effects of Our Fatherless Generation. Retrieved from https://krisvallotton.com/5-concerning-cultural-side-effects-of-our-fatherless-generation/

Across town, Paul engaged in a therapy session with Dr. Lynn. Marcia had recommended her to him. He'd been struggling emotionally, especially since being out of jail. He felt the lack of a father contributed to many of the dumb decisions he'd made in his life, and Paul never wanted to repeat or create new ones.

"Tell me what brought you in today, Paul?" Dr. Lynn asked, sitting in a chair facing him.

Paul nervously scratched the back of his head. Now that he was sitting in front of her, he didn't know where to begin.

"Okay, tell me a little about yourself," she offered, sensing his hesitation.

"I, ahhh—I recently got out of jail. I served a lil over a year of my six-year sentence for attempted armed robbery and carjacking. Marcia referred me; she and her husband are the ones I tried to rob that night. My friend and cellmate Ronny and I got pardoned a few months by the governor for our bravery for protecting some of the inmates and prison staff during a riot."

Dr. Lynn nodded. "I've heard about you on the news. That was courageous of you and your friend."

Paul smiled bashfully. "Thank you." He cleared his throat. "I, ahh—since I've been out, I'm continuing to pursue my bachelor's degree in accounting. I've also created a bookkeeping and tax app that's getting some attention. It's been keeping me afloat financially, and I'm working part-time at the college in the mailroom and offering to tutor in math."

Dr. Lynn smiled. "I'm impressed. You certainly break the stereotype of ex-cons that society seems to have. You prove all men locked up aren't bad guys, and you can learn from your mistakes and not repeat them."

"That's why I'm here. I've come to realize many of my problems and reasons I acted out were because I didn't know my father. And my mother died when I was a teenager. But even before my mom died, I felt lost. Like I was lacking. I needed attention and validation, and getting it from my mother wasn't enough. It didn't help that I sometimes got bullied in school for being a geek and oddball. My friend Bobby, who got locked up with me for the same charge, was the guy who fought my bullies for me. Since then, I've felt a sense of loyalty to him. It didn't matter, at the time, that he was involved in shady stuff. I stayed in trouble because of him.

My grades began to slip. I started skipping school to smoke weed, then stole snacks from the small convenience store around the corner from our neighborhood. I became the bully, roughing up kids, and stealing their lunch money, or whatever of value they had on them. All this landed me in jail because I followed Bobby's lead to carjack and rob two people we saw on the side of the road one rainy night. Now that I have my freedom, I don't want my daddy issues to cause me to do something stupid again. With prayer and faith, I made the best of my time in prison. Being sentenced was what I needed to get my head on straight, but I don't ever want to go back there."

"And you don't have to go back. You, Paul, control your destiny by the decisions you make. Have you ever watched the Ray Charles movie, acted by Jamie Foxx?"

Paul shook his head no.

"Well, one of the most memorable scenes in the movie was when Ray was in rehab, recovering from drugs. It was a painful time but necessary for his recovery. His drug addiction was a Band-Aid used to cover-up the real source of his pain. Ray felt he was the cause of his brother drowning as a child. For Ray to fully recover from drug addiction, he had to return to the source of his pain. Like Ray, I feel you need to go back to the source of your pain, which is the lack of a father. Because despite not having a father in your life, your life has a purpose; it has value. The guards spoke highly of you from the articles I've read. Even before you contacted me for therapy, I've been impressed with your story. You may not know your earthly father. But you have a heavenly father, and He's so in love with you, Paul. He wants the best for you. And like you said yourself, with faith and prayer, you made it through your time in prison. God was with you then, and He's with you now and forevermore. You have been twice pardoned, once by the governor, and by God. You have a second chance. Your past doesn't have to be your future."

Paul quickly wiped tears from his eyes. He nodded. "What can I do not to allow that lack to affect me again?"

"Continue what you've been doing since you've been in prison and released. Your life is on a positive path. Do you think you would've enrolled in college two years ago?"

Paul chuckled. "Probably not. I barely graduated high school with all the days I skipped and not putting much effort into my grades. I honestly hate to think what my life would've been had I not gotten arrested." He shook his head. "It sounds crazy, even saying that sometimes, but prison was a bad thing that turned out good in my favor."

"Because like Joseph, God was with you. Your faith in Him kept you. And I believe, like Joseph, your best days are ahead."

There was a consistent knock on Dr. Lynn's office door. The receptionist knew Dr. Lynn was meeting a client, and it was unlike her to interrupt. Dr. Lynn excused herself and went to answer the door.

"I'm sorry to interrupt. But the country is in a state of emergency. There have been reports of ten violent incidents all around the country, some right here in the DMV," the receptionist announced.

Dr. Lynn's mouth dropped open in shock. Paul shot to his feet. The receptionist barged into the office and clicked on the TV mounted on the wall. She quickly changed it to a news station reporting the incidents.

"God, help us!" Dr. Lynn shook her head in disbelief. "And all of this on the anniversary of 9-11."

Paul left the office, fishing for the cellphone in his pocket. He called Ronny. "Man, did you hear what's happening?"

"I was just about to call you. It's crazy out here. I was at the mall, and people started panicking when it was announced on loudspeakers that everyone had to evacuate in case of a potential attack. Sofia called," he said, referring to Officer Diaz, his girlfriend. "And told me her cousin was killed at the post office near the Pentagon."

Paul's heart sank. He was barely walking as a toddler on September 11, 2001. Here it was almost twenty years later, and this was happening. Terror, in the worse way. "That's sad. Please, give her my condolences."

"I will. I'm on my way to her now."

"Stay safe! It's crazy right now. I'm about to hit the road. I can only imagine it's chaotic." Paul unlocked his car and got in.

"Yeah. Traffic is a mess on the beltway, and it's not even rush hour traffic. I'll keep you posted. Check on your family."

"I am. I'll hit you up later." Paul ended the call and made another. "Hi, Marcia. Are you guys okay?"

"Hey, Paul. Yes, we're safe. We got the kids out of school early, and we're all home. Lisa and Karter are safe, as well. Are you okay?" she asked anxiously.

"I'm good. I was actually in a therapy session when Dr. Lynn and I received the news. I heard from Ronny, though. His girlfriend, Sofia's cousin, was killed in the shooting at the post office near the Pentagon."

"Oh, no! I'm so sorry to hear that. I will give him a call later. This is crazy what's happening."

"It is. You all stay safe. I have some more calls to make before I head home."

"Okay. Please, call me when you get home."

"Will do."

Chapter 30

"If my people, who are called by my name, will humble themselves and pray and seek my face and turn from their wicked ways, then I will hear from heaven, and I will forgive their sin and will heal their land." (2 Chronicles 7:14)

It's easy to blame someone else for the condition of the world. Collectively, we must all be responsible. Are we, as a society, responsible for some of the heartache, chaos, and pain we face in our world today? We can blame God; we can blame the president; we can blame Congress, but what if each person, in their own geographical areas, took personal responsibility for their own actions?

Michael Jackson was a popular singer in the mid-eighties until his death in 2009. Actually, he's still popular after death. He is known for his dancing as well as his singing, and his songs had incredible lyrics. One of my favorites is "Man in the Mirror." I encourage you to listen to the words. We first must look at ourselves in order to create change.

Interestingly, some people think the gun laws, or any other laws, can cause real change. Those laws, unfortunately, can have loopholes. The shooter in Dayton, Ohio, had someone buy the ammunition for him, which means laws are limited. What can change these tragedies is a changed heart. The heart needs to change from hatred, prejudice, and anything that doesn't line up with the word of God.

God has given us the prescription for a healed land – humble ourselves, turn from our wicked ways, and seek His counsel. To understand how this works, we must be members of God's family; this only applies to believers. Jesus took twelve disciples and changed the course of history and eternity. How much more can we, as believers, do? I had a toothache I took some medicine for. Soon the medicine stopped easing the pain, and I went to the dentist. I was told I was treating the symptom, but I had an infection as the source of my pain. Likewise, laws only treat the symptoms of evil. Jesus' type of love is the answer. The greatest commandment is to love your neighbor as yourself. I believe 99 percent of the world's problems would be solved if this commandment was followed.

The gas gauge blinked, indicating Ronny needed to stop for gas immediately, or he'd be walking. After getting the call from Sofia about her cousin being killed in one of the attacks, all he thought about was getting to her.

When it was safe to do so, he merged off the highway at the first exit. One of the local gas stations he frequented was a couple of turns away. He was familiar with the owner, Mr. Patel. Since he was a little boy, Mr. Patel was always nice to him and his parents whenever they visited. Mr. Patel, or his wife, would give him free candy or cookies that Ronny looked forward to as a child. The fact that Mr. and Mrs. Patel weren't white never dawned on Ronny; they were just nice people in his eyes. Until recently, he only saw Hispanics as different. He was thankful he no longer carried prejudice.

Ronny parked at a vacant pump, went inside to pay, and pick up some snacks for Sofia.

"Hello, Mr. Patel, how are you doing today?" Ronny asked upon entry, seeing the older gentleman standing behind the counter.

Mr. Patel waved. "I'm fine, Ronny. It's good to see you again since you've been released. My wife and I know you are a good boy who made a bad mistake. We all make bad mistakes sometimes. Just learn from them." He replied in his Middle Eastern accent. "You became a hero in prison and got pardoned. We are so proud of you!"

Ronny smiled bashfully. "Thank you, Mr. Patel. How is your wife?"

"She is fine; she just needed a day off. Standing all day on her feet isn't easy for her anymore."

Ronny nodded. The smell of the pizza made him hungry. "Is the pizza almost ready?"

"Almost."

Ronny went to pick up a few things for Sofia. A group of forty-five white males in their twenties and early thirties walked in the store. While looking over one of the low shelves, Ronny noticed his cousin Tim among the men.

"Hey, Tim. I haven't seen you in a while. How are you doing?"

Tim went over to Ronny. "Have you heard the news?" He asked, ignoring Ronny's question. "The country is under attack, again. On 9-11. The immigrants have infested our community and are destroying our country. The Middle Easterners attacked us eighteen years ago, but we're not going to sit back and let them do it again."

Ronny noticed the men getting rowdy, talking loudly and knocking items off shelves. "What are you talking about? And what are you planning to do? Nine-eleven was because of Al-Qaeda, Osama bin Laden. He was from Saudi Arabia. Mr. Patel is from India. And we don't know who is involved in these new attacks."

"Look who's talking; you tried to kill Hispanics." Tim sneered.

"Yes, that was a big mistake, and I paid my price. Please, don't hurt Mr. Patel. He's innocent, and he's my friend."

"He ain't no friend of ours." Tim raised his hand, sending the rowdy men loose, ransacking the place.

They knocked over shelves, broke the glass doors to the refrigerators lined up against one wall, broke apart displays, smashed merchandise. All while one man held Mr. Patel with his hands behind his back, watching in fear and horror as his place of business was destroyed.

One of the men yelled, "Let's get the money out of the register!"

"Please, don't do this! Tim, Make them stop."

Tim turned to look at Ronny. "They come into our country and steal our jobs and now more terrorist attacks."

"We don't know who's to blame. This is crazy. Please, stop! The FBI and Homeland Security are working to figure out who's to blame. Cousin, these are innocent people. Don't make things worse. You and these men are no different from the terrorist. This is hatred!"

Something Ronny said must've made sense because Tim told his buddies, "Let's go! Let's get out of here!"

They started to leave but not before grabbing snacks for the road.

Mr. Patel was in a state of shock. He held his head in agony at the destruction.

"Are you okay?" Ronny carefully walked closer to Mr. Patel.

"Yes, son, thank you so much. I told you; you are a hero. These things can be replaced. My life is more precious. I'm going to call the cops. Then I can start cleaning up."

"I will help you. I just need to make a call first."

***

"Babe, come! The president is about to address the nation," Thomas called out to Marcia.

She entered their bedroom belly first. Jada and James followed behind, and all found a spot to sit on the king-size bed.

Thomas picked up the remote and turned up the volume.

President Johnson wore a black suit with a light blue tie, sitting behind his desk in the Oval Office. "My fellow Americans, good evening. Today, as we remembered what happened eighteen years ago, we were faced again with cowardly acts of terrorism, hatred, and bitterness against the freedom we have fought hard to maintain. At 10 a.m., there were ten violent attacks in Florida, Virginia, D.C., New York, Ohio, Washington State, Maryland, and South Carolina.

We've had multiple attacks against American citizens today, mainly Hispanics and African Americans. Unfortunately, and consequently, some people have taken out their frustration about today's attack on people of Middle Eastern descent. Some innocent cab drivers, restaurant owners, and convenience store owners were viciously attacked in retaliation. Not only are we potentially dealing with foreign terrorism but domestic as well."

Scrolling at the bottom of the TV screen: *Breaking News! Breaking News! Three white male*

American suspects have been captured in the van attack in Florida.

"If I can dare compare, this is like Pearl Harbor and another nine-eleven combined in our country today," the president continued. "The country is in complete chaos with citizens turning against each other. We cannot hurt other American citizens –other humans. If anyone caught and convicted of threatening, killing, or harming any person because of their race, religion, or creed will be prosecuted to the full extent of the law. The FBI and Homeland Security are putting the pieces of this together. We don't know exactly what has happened and who is behind this, so we need your patience; we need your support, and we need America to be strong. Please don't take the law into your own hands."

Scrolling at the bottom of the TV screen: *Breaking News! Breaking News! Several groups of men throughout the country have been arrested for attacking and even killing Middle Easterners for no apparent reason.*

"Because of the chaos, fear, and anxiety in our country due to these events, I will sign an executive order declaring martial law until further notice. To see the evil and hatred inflicted on each other in the name of justice is heartbreaking. America, we are better than this." President Johnson shook his head. "But now, I must take personal responsibility for some of the hateful rhetoric I've said in the past. One of the captured suspects said he wanted to make America great again by stopping the infestation of immigrants and stopping caravan illegals from entering our country because Mexico only gives us drug dealers, rapists, and murderers.

As you all know, I have said these things. My method and motives were wrong. I take responsibility for the things I've said and the things I've done. I was wrong. Every human being is created in the image of God. We are all equal in the eyes of God. And now, too, in my eyes. All my life, I have been self-sufficient. I have never needed anyone. I've never truly apologized to anyone either. A few weeks ago, I accepted God's friend request and accepted Jesus Christ as my Lord and Savior.

I cannot undo the past. But I can change the future. With my son almost dying, my daughter being sick, and the political and criminal charges I'm facing, I need a savior, and His name is Jesus. The Bible says, 'What does it profit a man to gain the whole world and lose his soul.' So, my fellow Americans, I urge you all tonight to treat your neighbor as you would want to be treated."

Chapter 31

"And what do you benefit if you gain the whole world but lose your own soul? " (Mark 8:36)

If I were told I only had six months to live, I would only be concerned about significant things: my children, my wife. I want my family to be secured. I want them to succeed when I'm gone. Trouble has a way of causing us to become focused on the things that have or should have significance. I'm learning that success isn't what I thought it was – money, status, popularity, and approval from my peers. Rather success is fulfilling my godly purpose in life. If I had six months to live, I would make sure my will was intact, and my life insurance was current. Insurance guarantees the ones I care for will be provided for after my death.

Insurance doesn't guarantee we won't have accidents or death, but in the event something like that happens, insurance helps to replace or sustain us for what we have lost. Spiritually speaking, when we accept Jesus as our personal Savior, we have blessed insurance we can't buy, sell or trade. Our blessed insurance guarantees that we will receive the benefits of Christ's death. We have access to His kingdom.

Many, like myself in the past, often confuse success with fame, fortune, and money. However, as believers in Christ, we must seek the Savior and not worldly success. If

we are not sensitive to what the Lord is telling us, we may seek success not sanctioned by the Lord, which will only lead to our downfall.

Today was a sobering day for Sofia Diaz, her family, and many other people in the DMV area, around the country, and the world. A mass funeral was being held today for the three victims killed at the shooting at the post office. In all, twenty-three people were killed, and many others injured in the series of simultaneous attacks around the country less than a week ago.

Diaz's cousin was one of the victims. Ronny took Sofia's hand into his, clasping them together as they took the short steps leading into the megachurch. The church was in Prince Georges County, Maryland. The parking lot and entrance to the church were swarming with people coming to pay their last respects, the news media, and government officials. Among the crowd were many celebrities like Oprah Winfrey, Bill Gates, Tyler Perry, Serena Williams, Jay Z, and Beyoncé, even former presidents Jimmy Carter and Barack Obama, along with former first lady Michelle Obama. After they made it into the large lobby of the church, they met Marcia, Thomas, Jada, James, Lisa, and Karter awaiting their arrival.

"We're so sorry for your loss," Marcia said, hugging Sofia. The group took turns giving her a hug and their condolences. Karter and Lisa were properly introduced to Sofia and Ronny for the first time.

Sofia soberly stated. "Thank you; I appreciate you all for coming."

"Hey, sorry, I'm late. It took forever to find parking," Paul said, joining the group. He gave his condolences to Sofia, then greeted everyone else.

Thomas introduced his son Karter to Paul.

Marcia pulled away from hugging Paul. "You've never met my daughter Lisa. She's home for a short visit."

Paul turned to greet Lisa, outstretching his hand. "It's nice to meet you."

Lisa blinked a few times, lost in her own thoughts about how handsome Paul was. He smirked when Marcia nudged her with an elbow to say something. "Oh, yeah. Hi." Lisa shook his hand quickly, kicking herself for possibly looking like an idiot.

Paul thought she was cute but left his thought at that. They all entered the sanctuary, thankful to find seats where they all sat together.

Bishop Forbes and Pastor Brent Nelson were officiating the service. President Johnson reached out to them to do so. Pastor Brent was trying hard not to be nervous. He'd never preached in a church filled with 18,000 people and being watched by millions worldwide. *Use me to do Your will, Lord.* Pastor Nelson silently prayed, taking his seat next to Bishop, the president, first lady, and other government officials at the front of the church with the three closed caskets.

After the praise and worship led by Kirk Franklin and the prayer by Pastor Nelson, Bishop Forbes stepped to the podium. "I would like to express my condolences to the families who are mourning a loved one today. Hatred has won the battle today through senseless acts of murder. But I am declaring to you that love has won the war. The same way light is greater than darkness, love is the only thing that can overcome these evil acts of hatred and bitterness."

A male interpreter translated what was being said into Spanish.

Bishop continued. "I would like to thank our president and first lady for being here today on this great day of sadness."

Someone called out, "Bigot!"

"He's the reason why this tragedy happened!" A Hispanic lady in the back with a sharp accent yelled. "You wanted to make America great again! And look what you did! This is your fault!"

President Johnson stared ahead, trying not to let the outbursts bother him. He had prepared himself for such verbal attacks.

"I understand many are angry, but we're here to mourn these people's death, not bash the president," Bishop said.

The two people stopped their irate words toward the president.

Bishop asked everyone to stand and turn their Bibles or apps to the New Life Version, Revelation 7:9: "After this, I saw many people. No one could tell how many there were. They were from every nation and every family and every kind of people and every language. They were standing before the throne and before the Lamb. They were wearing white clothes, and they held branches in their hands."

Afterward, he instructed everyone to turn to the Message's version of Acts 10:28-30: "Peter said to them, You know it is against our Law for a Jew to visit a person of another nation. But God has shown me I should not say that any man is unclean. For this reason, I came as soon as you sent for me. But I want to ask you why you sent for me? Cornelius said, Four days ago, at three o'clock in the afternoon, I was praying here at my house. All at once, I saw a man standing in front of me. He wore bright clothes."

After the reading of the Scripture, everyone took their seats.

"There are three points I want to share with you. One, we are all made from the same maker. Many years ago, I went to the salvaged yard to get a fender for my red, 2004, Ram 2500 because the right fender had a lot of dents and began to rust. I asked the salesperson, at the counter, if he had a right fender for my truck. He checked their inventory then replied yes.

The cost was $125. I paid for the fender and waited for someone to bring it to me. When the salesman brought it to me, I noticed the fender was gray and not red like my truck. He said, 'It's a different color but made by the same manufacturer. So don't worry because it will fit.'"

The congregation was fully engrossed in his story.

"We may look different, sound different, we may be from different parts of the world, but we are all made by the same manufacturer. We are all made in the image of God. The color of the fender didn't matter. The fact that the fender was compatible with my truck is what mattered. A Chevy fender won't work on a Dodge truck. This is because they're two different kinds of trucks, made by two different manufacturers. Did you know that in heaven, there is no segregation? Also, did you know in heaven, there are multiple languages?"

Sofia reached over and grasped Ronny's hand, thankful he no longer saw Hispanics as inferior. If he hadn't given his life to Christ, they might not have become a couple. She loved him dearly and knew he felt the same about her. Ronny looked at her with a smile.

"Point two, we are accepted unconditionally by God, regardless of our race, language, or nationality. In Revelation 7:9: John said he saw a number that no man could count, and he saw every nation, every tongue, and every tribe in heaven. This means if you don't like me now, you won't like me when we get to heaven. This is why we must be born again or born from above. Every human being born into the earth is prequalified to become a citizen of heaven. The phrase "friend request" has become popular now, but all you have to do is say "yes" to Jesus.

Point number three, the power to change our generation begins with you. Facts can change. For instance, some laws have changed. There was a time when it was illegal for certain minorities to vote. It was legal for certain people to own other human beings. These facts were supported by the government. In 1863, Abraham Lincoln signed the Emancipation Proclamation. It declared that no human being had the right to own another human being.

Two thousand years ago, Christ came. He did more than liberate us physically; He also liberated us spiritually. Now He wants us to make disciples of others so that we can bring the good news to the ends of the earth. It takes courage to change our generation and to stand up against tradition, injustice, and unjust laws. How do we deal with racism from a biblical perspective? What does the Bible say about racism? Before there was prejudice between blacks and whites, racism and segregation existed in biblical times between Jews and Gentiles. Jews were proud people. It was unlawful for Jews to have fellowship with Gentiles.

Is it ever okay to disobey civil law? This question may be tricky, but I need your full attention. When civil law violates God's higher law, for example, the Bible states that we are to love our neighbors as ourselves, we have the authority of God to follow Him instead of unjust civil laws. In the Scripture we read in Acts, it was unlawful for Peter to enter into the house of a Gentile, but Peter went to Cornelius' house anyway, despite the laws and customs of men at that time. He chose to follow God and not man.

It takes courage to stand alone sometimes and do what God has commanded us to do. During the height of the civil rights movement, many white people were prosecuted and mistreated, spat on, whipped, hung, had dogs turned on them like the blacks they were defending and standing with for justice. Even before the civil rights movement, there were many abolitionists, during slavery, fighting for change. Today, I'm asking you to be filled with God's courage to take a stand for what is true: all men are created equal. God always uses a small group of people to make great changes. The question is, will you be part of the groups making change?"

Bishop turned the microphone over to Pastor Nelson, who continued with the eulogy for the three victims. Everyone was touched by their words and the memories shared of the victims by family and friends.

Nelson looked to the congregation. "Now, I give the podium to the president of the United States, Calvin Johnson."

At the podium, President Johnson wiped away a tear, pausing to gain composure. "I gave my condolences individually to the families here today, and I want to say it again publicly. I'm sorry for the loss of your loved one." His voice was filled with remorse. "It is my desire today will be a turning point in our country, and these lives that were lost were not lost in vain. Those responsible for the recent tragedies will pay the ultimate price for what they have done to you and our country.

Racism, hatred, and bitterness is a learned behavior. Babies are not born with it. Anything learned can be relearned. I want to apologize to the families who have suffered loss, to my great country, and the world at large for my role in these recent attacks. I feel I'm partly to blame for my past ignorance regarding the words I've said or written negatively of people of other races, nationalities, and religions. I was wrong. I know that now. I sincerely apologize. I stand before you as a changed man. I may look the same and sound the same, but my heart, my mind, and my will have submitted to a greater power. Jesus Christ, my Lord and Savior."

There were audible gasps at his words. Bishop and Nelson smiled happily at the president's words.

Johnson continued. "I can't take back the things I've said and done, but from this day forward, anything I say or do, I want it to glorify my Lord and Savior Jesus Christ. I have read the book *Journey to Faith*, and I have been on the journey ever since. As I close, I want to use the famous quote by Dr. Martin Luther King Jr." He paused, then continued. "We, as a country, have some difficult days ahead. But it doesn't matter to me now because I've been to the mountaintop. And I've seen the promised land, but I may not get there with you. If I could do things all over again, I would want to build bridges instead of walls. God bless you!"

The congregation erupted in applause.

Bishop Forbes returned to the podium. "Hate has united us here today, but love will keep us united beyond this day. I hope what was said today won't be forgotten, but if there's one thing I hope you remember, it's this!"

Lights dimmed; then, the stage lit up, showcasing a star cast of singers and performers: Usher, Fantasia, Yolanda Adams, Peabo Bryson, Donnie McClurkin, Mariah Carey, and a few others, singing, "We Are the World."

Chapter 32

"God does not see you as a Jew or as a Greek. He does not see you as a servant or as a person free to work. He does not see you as a man or as a woman. You are all one in Christ." (Galatians 3:28)

I want to paraphrase the verse above to read: In Christ, there is neither black or white; there is neither rich or poor, male or female. No one is preferred over another; we are all equal in Him.

What does the Bible say about interracial relationships? Is It biblical? How do you feel about interracial relationships? Ask yourself this question: If your child or a close friend or relative came to you and said they were dating a Christian of another race, how would you feel? This is a tough question for some people. Besides whether the person is good for them, my concern would be the scrutiny they might face, including the looks, comments, and maybe even attacks.

In 2 Corinthians 6:1:4: the Bible speaks about not being unequally yoked, meaning that one person is a believer and the other isn't. As long as both parties are of Christian faith, there are no biblical issues with interracial marriage.

Growing up, some of the parents of my white friends were vocal about their disagreement with interracial marriage. I slept over at their house, ate with them, but they were against mixed-raced relationships.

As we see in the story, Marcia wasn't looking for a white man. Marcia was looking for a godly man. In Deuteronomy 7:1-6: God told the Israelites not to marry the people of Canaan. It wasn't because they were of a different race; it was because they were of a different faith. "For they will turn your sons away from following Me to serve other gods."

Even King Solomon dealt with the pressures of loving women of different races, but this was God's warning in 1 Kings 11:2: "They were from the nations about which the Lord had said to the people of Israel, 'Do not take wives from them. And do not have them take wives from you. For they will be sure to turn your heart away to follow their gods.' Again, God's warning wasn't because of their race; it was because of their faith. Moses' wife was of a different nationality/race. He married an Ethiopian woman (a Cushite woman). His brother Aaron and sister Miriam were against his marriage. God rebuked both and punished Miriam, making her white as snow with leprosy she had to endure for seven days. If God wasn't upset with Moses for marrying someone of a different race, why would He be upset if people chose to do so today? If God isn't against interracial marriage, why should we?

Marcia was thirty-five weeks pregnant and over it. She was ready to have her body back all to herself.

Their son and daughter were wreaking havoc on her bladder, bouncing on it like it was an exercise ball. Her belly was huge, so she knew they were running out of room in there. Marcia's doctor gave her two more weeks before she would be ready to deliver to reduce the risk of stillbirth and newborn death.

Marcia was excited about the getaway, or babymoon, to West Virginia at a lodge cabin resort, surrounding Stonewall Jackson Lake. Thomas had rented a small RV for the trip, allowing Marcia to recline and relax during the five-hour drive. The resort was breathtakingly beautiful, especially the views of the lake.

They enjoyed four days of being out on the water on a boat, not far from shore. Thomas fished, and Marcia enjoyed the quiet while reading a novel. They went sightseeing, enjoyed time at the spa, and relaxed in the pool. Now they were headed back home. They were four hours into the drive when they decided to stop for lunch at a cute little restaurant they discovered on their drive down.

"I'm always hungry," Marcia vented, rubbing her belly. They were seated and already placed their order for club sandwiches, a salad, and fresh lemonade.

"Because you're eating for three." Thomas placed his arm around Marcia's shoulder, kissing her on the forehead.

"There goes one of them agreeing with you." She looked down at her belly, which resembled a mouse running underneath her shirt.

"It's so surreal seeing them do that." Thomas placed a hand on her belly. He felt one of the babies move. "Don't worry, kiddos; you will be out of their soon. We have your new room waiting for you."

"It's bad enough you're an interracial couple, did y'all have to bring an innocent baby in the mix?" A disgruntled voice said.

Thomas sat up straighter, turning to lock eyes with the man stopping by their table.

"What my wife and I do is none of your business!" Thomas spat. Occasionally, he and Marcia received curious looks from people, depending on where they were. But this was the first time someone had expressed their displeasure toward them.

"Y'all in my line of sight, so that makes it my business," the middle-aged white man said with a southern drawl.

Thomas stood with Marcia tugging on his arm. "You need to stop with the disrespect! My wife and I just want to enjoy a peaceful lunch and not listen to your ignorance."

The man pointed his scrawny finger. "Enjoy it somewhere ..."

"That's enough, Jessie! I told you before if you disrespect any of my customers again, you're banned. Now get out! I've called the police, and I'm sure they'll be on the lookout for you, again," said the burly white man, appearing to be in his mid-sixties, wearing an apron.

"I don't need to eat from your black loving behind no way!" Jessie spat before walking out of the restaurant.

"I'm Matt, the owner," he said, extending a hand to Thomas. "I apologize for that. Jessie's a drunk who gets on his high horse, starting an ignorant crusade. He's been in and out of jail for his racist remarks; soon he'll stay there for good if he keeps up."

It took Thomas a moment before responding. He was still processing what just happened. He shook Matt's hand. "Thanks for the apology. I'm Thomas," he said, turning to Marcia, "and this is my beautiful wife, Marcia."

"Hi," Marcia replied, rubbing her belly.

"Again, I'm sorry about what just happened. Please, let me make it up a little by taking care of your bill."

Thomas shook his head. "No, you don't have to."

"I know I don't, but I would appreciate it if you allowed me to. Many of the people in this town and I don't agree with Jessie. I don't want you thinking we're all like him. And I want to because it's a nice thing to do."

"Thank you." Thomas accepted.

"We appreciate it," Marcia chimed in.

"Marcia, are you okay?" Thomas asked, looking at his wife from the rearview mirror. She was reclining on the couch in the RV displaying a grimace. They decided to take their food to go after the incident with Jessie. Marcia didn't feel comfortable being there anymore, and Thomas was afraid the stress of the incident would affect her and the babies. "Should I call your doctor?"

"Ahhhhhh!" She screamed, clutching her hardening midsection.

Thomas almost skidded off the road from her declaration of pain. He refocused his attention on the highway ahead. His cellphone was mounted in front of him on the dashboard; he clicked a button and said, "Call, Doctor." Soon the call was connected to Dr. Adderley's personal cellphone. "Doc, I think Marcia is having contractions. We're about forty-five minutes from the hospital."

"Oh, my. I was hoping she would make it to thirty-seven weeks. But don't worry, I'll be there when you arrive," the doctor confirmed.

"I'm scared, Thomas," Marcia expressed through the tears. "It's—it's too soon for them. What if—what if –"

Thomas shook his head vigorously. "No what-ifs. You and our babies will be fine," he said, feeling her concern. "Everything will be fine. Dr. Adderley said he'll meet us at the hospital."

Thomas looked at the gauge; he was going sixty on a forty mile per hour road. Considering he needed to get to the hospital quickly, Thomas e made a left turn, and seconds later, he saw red and blue lights flashing in the rearview mirror. Impatiently, he pulled the RV over to the side of the road.

A cop cautiously walked up to the driver's side door. "Sir, you're driving mighty fast in this RV."

"Ben!" Thomas immediately recognized his former colleague from the Charles County Sheriff's Office. "My wife is in labor, and we need to get to the hospital now!" Thomas was trying not to panic.

Marcia let out a bloodcurdling scream. Ben and Thomas's eyes grew wide with concern.

"Follow me. I'll get you to the hospital quick." Ben ran back to his squad car, pulling it in front of Thomas to follow.

Thomas pulled the RV up to the emergency entrance of the hospital, like a scene out of a movie. Thankfully, Marcia had a tight grip on the couch and didn't fall off when he made the sharp turn.

"We made it, baby," he said, unbuckling his seatbelt and coming to her side.

The RV door opened, and Ben stepped in. "I have a wheelchair for her. I called ahead, and they're expecting her."

Thomas helped Marcia out of the RV and into the wheelchair, then started for the hospital doors.

"Hey, Thomas, you want me to park this for you?" Ben called out.

"Oh, yeah! Keys are in the ignition! Thanks, Ben!"

"Ahhh, sir, you may want to slow down," a nurse said from behind Thomas.

He looked over his shoulder. "I can't; my wife is in labor."

"Yeah, and labor and delivery are that way." She pointed to the left of her.

Thomas stopped abruptly with Marcia almost falling out of the wheelchair. She held her belly. "Remind me never to let you knock me up again."

The nurse smirked from having heard that line a time too many. Thomas pushed the wheelchair in the right direction with the nurse in the lead.

Marcia was groaning in pain, anxiously waiting for the meds the anesthesiologist administered to kick in. The anesthesiologist had left the room less than five minutes ago.

"It still hurts so bad," she whined with a death grip on the bedrail as a wave of contractions attacked her. Sweat beads formed on her forehead and rolled down to her neck.

Thomas picked up the cool towel, placed ice chips on it, and soothed it across Marcia's face and neck. "Breathe through the pain, baby. The doctor said the meds will take effect in a few more minutes."

"These babies are trying to kill me," she groaned. It was only her, Thomas, and a nurse in the room. The kids were on their way since she was progressively dilating. Marcia was five centimeters dilated and didn't think she would survive making it to ten. "I don't know how I did this three times before."

"You're doing well. Our babies will be here soon." Thomas kissed her lips.

"Just know, I'm getting on birth control until I finish menopause. I'm convinced you have super sperm." She croaked a laugh now that the contraction had passed. Thomas and the nurse laughed along with her.

Less than two hours later, they welcomed their son Tiaan, weighing six pounds and daughter Marlana, weighing five pounds. Both were eighteen inches long.

Thomas was in awe, holding his children as they slept in his arms. After giving birth, Marcia was able to breastfeed both of them before she succumbed to much-needed rest. Tiaan and Marlana were only an hour old and already captured his entire heart. The twins were fully developed and didn't need to be in the neonatal intensive care unit. Thomas was now a father of six and thanked God every moment for blessing him with his family. *Help me, Lord, to be the father You need me to be for all my children.* He raised the babies in his arms and kissed them on their foreheads.

Chapter 33

"He went on his way until he came near Damascus. All at once, he saw a light from heaven shining around him. He fell to the ground. Then he heard a voice say, "Saul, Saul, why are you working so hard against Me?" Saul answered, "Who are You, Lord?" He said, "I am Jesus, the One Whom you are working against. You hurt yourself by trying to hurt Me." Saul was shaken and surprised. Then he said, "What do You want me to do, Lord?" The Lord said to him, "Get up! Go into the city, and you will be told what to do." (Acts 9:3-6)

"Ananias said, But, Lord, many people have told me about this man. He is the reason many of Your followers in Jerusalem have had to suffer much. He came here with the right and the power from the head religious leaders to put everyone in chains who call on Your name. The Lord said to him, Go! This man is the one I have chosen to carry

My name among the people who are not Jews and to their kings and Jews. I will show him how much he will have to suffer because of Me. So, Ananias went to that house. He put his hands on Saul and said, "Brother Saul, the Lord Jesus has sent me to you. You saw the Lord along the road as you came here. The Lord has sent me so you might be able to see again and be filled with the Holy Spirit." (Acts 9:13-17)

God doesn't deal with us according to our past; He deals with us according to His eternal plan for us. God told

Ananias that Saul was a chosen vessel/instrument to carry His name to the Gentiles, kings, and the children of Israel. There are three things Ananias did that showed his amazing trust in God: 1. In spite of Saul's past, Ananias welcomed him into the body of Christ, calling him Brother Saul; 2. Ananias confirmed to Saul that Jesus appeared to him on the road to Damascus. There was no other way for him to know that unless Jesus also came to him in a vision; 3. Ananias laid hands on Saul, and Saul's sight was restored.

John Newton, writer of the song, "Amazing Grace," went from being a slave shipmaster, selling slaves, to becoming an abolitionist; one who spoke out against slavery. God took the thing he did for evil and made good out of it. John made a 360-degree turn in his perspective. Like Saul of Tarsus, we all must have a Damascus Road experience, where we meet our Savior, and instead of judgment, we find amazing grace. His grace will reveal truth and enable us to do with Him what we can't do without Him.

The very people Saul was killing; he was now laying down his life for. His name was later changed to Paul. He was the first theologian of the church. People were amazed that God used someone like Saul. I think God takes pleasure in using people that seem unlikely, unqualified. It greater emphasizes His power at work. God will use us not because of us but despite us. I would be careful to say who God cannot use to bring glory to His name.

Paul was happy to be home. It was a long day. Every time he came home, unlocking the door to his own apartment, he thanked God. It wasn't much, a 700 square foot, one-bedroom apartment with minimal furniture, but the place was his. He moved in a couple of weeks ago. Soon he would have the place completely furnished the way he wanted it. For now, he had a brand-new bedroom set and television. Lisa said she would go furniture shopping with him when he was ready and when she was in town on break from college. The two had gotten close since they'd met at the funeral.

Paul took his shoes off at the door to avoid tracking dirt on the carpet and made his way into the small kitchen to grab a bottled water. After entering his room, he picked up the remote and turned on the television before getting relaxed on the bed.

Jimmy Black's news show was on.

"Is this Watergate Two?" Jimmy asked. He started clapping dramatically. "Watergate was a scandal that occurred in 1972 with President Nixon. Three articles of impeachment were approved for Nixon. The first article was for obstruction of justice, the second was for abuse of power, and the third was for contempt of congress.

Nixon resigned from office on August 9, 1974. President Nixon also hated the news media. Can history repeat itself? Mr. President, when you get out of jail, you can win an Oscar for best actor as president of the United States. You put on one heck of a show at the funeral a few months ago, trying to convince us that you've changed from being a racist bigot to finding Jesus." Jimmy laughed. "Mr. Johnson, I almost want to believe you, but it's hard believing a zebra can change his stripes.

I remember your awful hate-filled tweets. How can you change? It is impossible to change. Now you're using religion as a crutch. You are trying to create a smokescreen. Your poll numbers are down. There's absolutely no way you're being reelected next month. You're having marital problems. And you're facing criminal charges."

Strolling at the bottom of the screen: *Breaking News: Speaker of the House has formally opened up an impeachment hearing for President Johnson for money he received from North Korea.*

"Tonight, I have with me in the studio, Pastor Brent Nelson; he is the author of the book *Journey to Faith* that President Johnson referred to reading.

Pastor Nelson was also one of the pastors who officiated the funeral for the terrorist attack victims in Maryland and D.C. Thanks for coming on to be a guest."

Pastor Nelson smiled when the camera was placed on him. "Thank you for inviting me on."

"Is it true that you're also one of the president's spiritual advisors?"

"I've met with him, and he's read my book, but I don't technically have that title."

"I've heard that you were with President Johnson when he gave his life to Christ. Can you confirm that?"

Nelson nodded. "Yes, that is true. He gave his life to Christ. He's a believer and follower of Jesus."

"So, you're telling me that God can forgive someone so evil. He claims to be a multimillionaire, but it's from beating people out of money. He's accused of taking bribes from the enemy. He is indirectly or rather directly responsible for what happened again on nine-eleven. We had multiple attacks in our country, and the attackers were motivated by him. They were trying to create a racial war. So again, I ask you, how can God change him?"

"No one is beyond God's grace. You seem self-righteous. I agree that some of what you said may be true about President Johnson, but if he has changed, isn't that a good thing."

"You mean a jailhouse conversion type thing?"

Nelson shook his head. "All I know is he seemed sincere. He admitted what he did was wrong. But what I want to know from you, Jimmy, is how can you judge someone's heart and motive? You're judging him on his past but not his present. The God of the Bible is a God of second chances, and all of us need second chances. There is a man in the Bible named Saul whose name was later changed to Paul. Saul prosecuted the church.

He hated the church, but God used him as an instrument to bring healing to the church. Later, he died for the church he was trying to prosecute. I can admit the president's transformation seems radical, but the God I serve is radical. Think about it; President Johnson is probably the most recognizable person in the world. His past is only a piece of many pieces to his life, and God has a plan for him as He has for all of us."

"You should receive the award for best supporting actor. I don't believe this crap; people don't change overnight. Rome wasn't built in a day."

"Yes, but people aren't cities, we're human beings. Surely, the creator of the heavens and earth can save to the outermost."

"Let me make sure I'm clear about this; you're saying God can change anyone? Can God change Adolf Hitler, Joseph Stalin, Saddam Hussein, David Koresh?"

"Absolutely. If they repent of their sins and accept God as their Lord and Savior, yes, they can change! The blood of Jesus reaches to the highest of heights and lowest of lows. Why is that so hard to believe? Love is stronger than hate; light is greater than darkness, and God's grace is greater than our sins."

"What about a person reaping what they have sown?" Jimmy asked.

"Yes, there are consequences for our actions, but that has nothing to do with our salvation. There is a parallel between spiritual birth and physical birth. We had nothing to do with either; it is a gift. Why it so hard for you to believe people can change?"

"I find it hard to believe a man like him can change from a snake to a sheep. All I know is proceedings have started for his impeachment, and I, like many people, look forward to him no longer being the president. If we're lucky, he goes to jail, too." Jimmy turned his attention to the monitor, looking directly at the screen. "Before we close, we polled a few people on the streets of D.C. to get their opinions about the president's Christian conversion. Take a look at this."

A clip played of a black woman, appearing to be in her forties with a microphone held in front of her. "Hi, Linda. What do you think about the president's conversion to Christianity?" The news reporter asked.

Linda replied, "I do believe God can change people, but I find it hard to believe the president found Jesus. It seems fishy he's talking about his Christianity now that he can possibly be impeached and go to jail. But I will reserve judgment. I know I won't be voting for him next month."

The same question was asked to Hosea, a Hispanic, thirty-something years old man. "Absolutely not! Some of my relatives have been deported because of that lunatic! He's only claiming Jesus because he's about to go to jail. I can't wait to vote next month."

The same question was also asked to Art, a burly tall white male in his early forties with a Swastika tattoo on his left forearm. "I do believe he has changed. I recall him saying, 'I may look the same and sound the same, but on the inside, I am different.' That really resonated with me. Actually, because of him, I have accepted Jesus as my personal Savior, and I am learning to love and look at people as God does. I quit my old gang and created a new gang called Angels of the Lord. We no longer represent the bigot and racist views we once had. Now we want to be disciples for Christ."

The news reporter asked Art, "Are you voting for him next month?"

"I am, but I doubt he's going to win."

Chapter 34

"For a child is born to us, a son is given to us. The government will rest on his shoulders. And he will be called: Wonderful Counselor, Mighty God, Everlasting Father, Prince of Peace." (Isaiah 9:6)

Whether we are Republicans, Democrats, or Independents, we are called to support and pray for our president and leaders, though sometimes it may be difficult. As believers, we are citizens of a greater kingdom, and we must reflect God's will and His purpose on the earth. It's easy to complain about our political leaders, but imagine how much time could be used praying for them instead of complaining? Love covers a multitude of sins. None of us are perfect, and we all require prayer and forgiveness from our Heavenly Father and one another. Our political leaders need our prayers, maybe now more than ever before.

President Johnson was sitting behind his desk in the Treaty Room in the White House when Vice President Clark walked in.

. "I've called you here today, Vice President, to let you know that after much thought regarding my political career and personal life, it's best to resign my position as the president of the United States. With reelection a month away, I know I won't be reelected. Most of the staff has given up on me, and I've let three of my loyal soldiers down. Two of my lawyers and my past Secretary of Defense are in jail today because of me. I want to pardon them before I resign. Matter of fact, it will be done today if they accept."

Vice President Clark replied, "When you told me about this a few months ago, I promised that if you resigned, I would pardon your crimes. I know you didn't come to this decision lightly."

"I didn't. In a few hours, I will be making a resignation speech. There's no sense in prolonging it any longer. Thank you for standing by my side."

Johnson stood, and they shook hands.

"Of course, I've got your back until the end," Clark assured him.

At seven that night, President Johnson sat in the Oval Office to give his resignation speech. He cleared his throat to help get rid of some of the nervousness right before the camera in front of him went live.

"Good evening, my fellow Americans. Over the last almost four years, I've had the incredible opportunity to be the president of this great country, the United States of America. There have been many highs and lows during my presidency. For these last few months, my life has gained a new perspective. I've become a true believer in the Lord and Savior, Jesus Christ.

All my life, I've been selfish, self-seeking, and self-serving. Many have questioned whether or not a person can truly change. I've asked myself that same question. From the moment I confessed Jesus as my Savior, my life became brand new. Biblical Scripture teaches us to judge a tree by the fruit it bears. Yes, I made many mistakes in the past, but to the best of my ability, with what influence I have left, with what money I have left, I will do like Zacchaeus did in the Bible. I have bragged about being a billionaire, and with becoming one, I've hurt many people and businesses in the process. But I want to rectify some of my wrongs.

I will set $500 million in an escrow account for anyone I defrauded, or I filed bankruptcy protection in order not to pay them what was owed. I will buy some buildings in the abandoned communities in Baltimore City, and other cities around the country to revitalize and establish low-income housing and jobs. I will also set up a fund to assist legal immigrants with court cases and assistance with locating and reuniting with their loved ones in detention centers. Also, the fund will assist with Americans needing assistance with obtaining U.S. visas for their loved ones in other countries. I will also establish a fund to provide awareness and cultural sensitivity training within major cities in America. On a personal level, my wife and I want to look into adopting a child from either Mexico or Haiti. And I feel lead to go on a missionary journey to several parts of the world to spread the gospel of Christ.

With all that being said, tonight is also really about me announcing my resignation as the president of the United States." President Johnson paused for a moment to regain his composure. "I have failed you as president, and I hope you will forgive me for not honorably upholding my position. It may seem odd that I'm choosing to resign just a month away from reelection, but I see no need to prolong my position. I no longer want to bring shame to you as a country by holding on to something I'm no longer worthy of keeping.

My family agrees with my decision to leave office, and I feel Vice President Clark will be best to carry out the last few months as president of the United States. I will resign my position of president effective at ten a.m. tomorrow. Vice President Clark will be sworn in as president after that. It has been a privilege to have been voted your president. Good night."

***

Former President Calvin Johnson paced the large and professionally decorated living room of his home in Philadelphia. He'd been residing there since leaving the White House. It had been a few weeks, and President Clark hadn't pardoned him yet and stopped the pending trial for taking money from North Korea.

The country elected its first black female president, Cordella Simms. Her swearing-in was coming up soon, and Calvin was worried he wouldn't get his pardon in time from President Clark.

He stared at his cellphone, anxiously willing it to ring. He called and left countless messages for President Clark and hadn't received a returned call.

"It would be quite a dilemma for secret service to guard a former president in prison," Camilla said, taking a seat on the couch. She watched her husband pace the marble floors.

"Not now, Camilla. Please."

"I'm sorry. I was just trying to make light of the situation."

"It's not helping."

His cellphone rang. He instantly picked it up from the coffee table. It was the call he'd been waiting for.

"President Clark."

"Sorry, I'm just now returning your call."

"What's taken you so long? I thought you would've pardoned me by now, so I can put this case behind me."

The line went dead for a moment. "I've had a change of heart. I've decided that since your recent conversion to Christ and your willingness to right your wrongs, you should go to trial and await your judgment. Wouldn't it be the Jesus thing to do?"

Johnson's mouth hung open in shock. "After everything I've done for you, you'll do that to me?"

Clark laughed bitterly. "If you really wanted to do me a favor, you should've resigned sooner. My political career is over because of you, but I'll enjoy my last few weeks as commander-in-chief. Enjoy prison."

The call ended.

"What did he say?" Camilla asked.

"I'm going to trial."

It was a media frenzy inside and out of the courthouse. Resigned former President Calvin Johnson never in his life thought he would be standing before a judge to plead his case and await his faith. He went from being president of a great nation to facing maybe the rest of his life in prison.

But his newfound faith in God didn't waver. He was at peace that he was able to correct some of his wrongs before he spent the rest of his life behind bars. He accepted a bribe from North Korea. The money helped his campaign and axed out the credibility of his opponent. It helped him get elected. In exchange, he was going to loosen up on some sanctions against North Korea. He hadn't followed through on his end of the deal, which was why leaks of the deal were revealed. He loved America too much to have betrayed the American people in that way.

"The Lord is my Shepherd," Johnson silently prayed the 23 Psalms he'd memorized a few weeks ago. His lawyers sat to the left and the right of him. His wife Camilla, daughter Ava, and son Oscar were sitting behind him in support.

He knew the Democrats wanted him to pay and, their case was stacked high against him. The phone call leaks were enough. All his defense had was that he didn't follow through on his end of the North Korean deal.

The courtroom began to settle, and everyone showed respect when the judge entered the room and took her place at the bench.

"Well, this is interesting," the judge said once everyone was seated. "Resigned President Johnson, it's been brought to my attention that there may not be a trial today."

There were shocked expressions in the courtroom. Johnson sat completely confused. His lawyers looked at each other, wondering if they'd missed a memo.

"Democratic President Cordella Simms has granted you pardon. Do you accept?"

There were some shouts of outrage and some of awe and shock at her words.

Johnson had never been more surprised in his entire life. His opponent had granted him pardon. *Jesus, thank You!* It took him a moment to fully comprehend what was offered.

"Yes! Yes! I accept."

"Okay. You're free to go."

The media went wild. Reporters were frantically asking questions and cameras were flashing rapidly.

Chapter 35

"Your love for one another will prove to the world that you are my disciples." (John 13:35)

How can we truly know if a person has changed? An apple tree can only be considered an apple tree if it produces apples. A Christian is defined as a person who accepts Jesus as their Lord and Savior and lives a life that reflects Him. Jesus never physically hurt anyone. Jesus was never part of a political takeover. He never spoke ill of the rulers of His day. He commanded His disciples to bring healing to the world and to love their neighbors as they loved themselves. You can't say you love God and hate your neighbor. It's a contradiction. Hatred, bitterness, racial superiority, is a fruit that is seen. The evidence of a believer is to act like their Savior. An apple can only produce an apple. Hate can only produce hate. The act of love is the only way to confirm someone has truly changed.

"I think we go through a pack of diapers a day," Marcia vented. She was in the passenger seat while Thomas drove. The twins were behind them asleep in their baby car seats.

"And two packs of wipes," Thomas added. "But they are the most adorable little poop masters." He chuckled, and Marcia joined in.

"They are. Anything else you can think of that we need from the store?" She was making a list.

"Nope, I think you got everything. Oh, wait! Jada wants blueberry Pop-Tarts." They arrived at the grocery store, and he parked.

"I'll shop while you watch the babies. There's no need for us to wake them." Marcia gathered her purse.

"Okay."

"Should take me thirty minutes."

Marcia got a cart and quickly got all the items on her list. She knew they had maybe forty minutes before the twins would wake up to eat. Marcia hoped they made it home by then. Once everything on her list was piled in the cart, she got in line to check out. Marcia wished the self-checkout line wasn't down so she could've gotten out of there sooner.

"I'm sorry, sir, but your card was declined."

Marcia looked up from browsing on social media on her phone. The man, one place ahead of her, nervously looked through his wallet for another card to swipe.

"I'd like to pay for your things if you don't mind," Marcia said, excusing herself from the woman in front of her.

The young man looked pleasantly surprised and grateful for her offer. "Thanks, but you don't have to. I'll just put some things back."

"I don't have to, but I would like to do it for you. Someone did the same for me once at this same grocery store, and I would like to return the favor to you."

The young man's eyes were filled with emotion. "Thank you! I really appreciate it."

Marcia took out her credit card and paid for his items. Afterward, she hugged him goodbye and a witness card to her church.

After paying for her own items, Marcia headed to the SUV, where Thomas was waiting. He got out as she approached, and helped put the groceries in the trunk.

"Why do you have that silly grin on your face?" Thomas asked, loading the trunk.

"I paid for a young man's groceries. His card was declined, and he would've had to put some items back. He was me not too long ago."

Thomas smiled, remembering the first time they met. Who would've thought that today, they would be married and have twins. *God you are awesome!* "God has blessed us tremendously since then, and it's a blessing for you to pass the kindness on."

"Yeah, I pray it becomes a domino effect."

Before closing the trunk. he kissed her on the forehead.

"Let's get home before the twins wake up."

Kirk Franklin's song "Give Me" featuring Mali Music was playing on the radio. Marcia and Thomas began singing along to the song. But not loud enough to wake the babies up.

Thomas made his usual turn from the grocery store to go home onto a secondary road while they continue singing. Moments later, the SUV started to pull to one side; then, they heard a loud pop.

Thomas realized one of the tires must have blown out. The secondary road didn't have much of a shoulder to pull onto, but he did the best he could while driving a Chevy Tahoe. He put the hazard lights on and got out to inspect the damage. As he guessed, the back right tire had blown out. He went to the trunk to prepare to change the tire and realized something else.

"I must have driven over something earlier today because these tires are new," Thomas said after returning to the driver's seat. "Now, do you want the good news or bad news first?"

"Bad news. Always start with the bad news first."

"Bad news is the jack is defective. I meant to buy a new one but forgot. The good news is we have a spare." He was kicking himself for not being properly prepared for a flat tire with his family.

He got his phone to look for the number for roadside assistance. A horn blew loudly, jarring them, and it woke the twins up. They started crying.

"I almost crashed into you!" An irate woman said, rolling down her window. Her car was alongside theirs.

"Sorry, we have a flat tire. Do you have a carjack we can use?" Thomas asked.

"Yeah, but I don't know you. Sorry, bye." She drove off.

Marcia climbed over the console, got in the back, and sat between the twins trying to soothe their cries. They settled down a bit at the sound and sight of their mother.

"A truck won't be able to get here for an hour," Thomas said. He shook his head in frustration. He could walk a few miles back to the gas station they passed and get a jack, but he didn't want to leave Marcia and the babies there alone.

The twins started to whine more. Marcia passed their daughter to him then took their son out of his car seat. She handed Thomas a bottle of breastmilk to feed Marlana; then, she fed Tiaan.

The roar of motorcycles could be heard before they were seen. Thomas looked in the rearview mirror and saw more than five people on motorcycles headed their way. They looked to be part of a gang. Naturally, he became alarmed. He didn't have his service weapon, and he didn't like the vulnerability he was feeling with being unarmed if he had to defend his family.

The men on the bikes stopped right behind them. Marcia looked over her shoulder out the back window, praying they meant no harm.

Thomas passed Marlana back to Marcia to burp. "I'm going to see what they want."

"Okay," she nervously replied.

Thomas met the men at the rear of the SUV.

"Hey, you need some help?" A burly tall white male, appearing to be in his early forties with a cross tattooed on his forearm, asked Thomas.

"Yes, one of our tires blew out. You wouldn't happen to have a carjack on your chopper, would you?" Thomas asked jokingly. It helped relieve some of the tension with the whole situation.

The man laughed. "I'm Art, and this is my gang Angels of the Lord. We don't carry carjacks, but one of us can go and get one for you. The rest of us can help prevent cars from running into you parked on the side of the road like this."

Thomas knew God worked in mysterious ways, but he was still shocked and extremely grateful for Art's kindness.

It took one of the men in the gang twenty minutes to purchase and return with a carjack.

Thomas offered to pay for it, but Art and his crew refused. In no time, the men had the car jacked up, flat tire removed, and spare tire screwed on safely.

"Thank you so much for helping us," Marcia said to the men.

"Yes, thank you! Honestly, when I saw you all approaching, I wasn't too sure of what you guys would do."

"If this were a year ago, we wouldn't have been too friendly, especially you being a white man with a black woman. But being a true supporter of President Johnson and when he gave his life to Christ, we became convicted and found the Lord ourselves. Now our gang is the Angel of the Lord to spread God's kindness and grace."

"I guess people can truly change," Marcia commented.

"Indeed." Art said, getting on his chopper and riding off with his gang.

Epilogue

Sixteen months later.

Former President Calvin Johnson fulfilled all the promises he made during his resignation speech. Three months after being pardoned, he and his wife, Camilla, adopted a four-year-old girl from Haiti. Little Roseline is a new joy to their lives. Calvin enjoys his work in the mission fields helping the less fortunate and spreading the love of Christ – he's found a new fulfillment in life.

Pastor Brent Nelson's church had grown to thirty-five hundred members in one year and is still growing. This was due to the international spotlight he received from being one of the pastors who officiated the funeral for the terrorist attack victims in Maryland and D.C, and his book *Journey to Faith* being on the New York Times Best Sellers List. The term he used in his book, *accepting God's friend request*, had become internationally known.

Pastor Nelson's secretary, Francine, a black woman in her early forties, barged into his office. Nelson looked up from his computer screen with a perplexed look on his face.

"Pastor Nelson, there's a man on the phone for you that said he's Tyler Perry. I've watched many Tyler Perry movies and he sounds nothing like Madea." Francine placed a hand on her hip while holding the doorknob with her other hand.

Nelson rubbed his chin in thought wondering if maybe it's a prank call. "Okay, what extension is he on?" He went to reach for the phone on his desk.

"Two."

Nelson picked up the phone hitting extension two. "This is Pastor Nelson speaking, how can I help you?"

"Pastor Brent Nelson, it's a pleasure to speak with you sir. I'm Tyler Perry."

Despite what Francine said it sounded like Tyler Perry to Nelson. He tried his best to pipe down his excitement. "Mr. Perry, wow. How can I assist you?"

"The influence your book Journey to Faith has had on former President Johnson and countless others, I'm interested in making it into a movie."

Whaaaaattttt! Nelson was speechless. *Dear God, is this real?* Francine was still anxiously standing at the office door only hearing Nelson's side of the conversation.

"Pastor Nelson, are you still there?"

"Yes, yes. Ahhh, I will be honored for you to make my book and the influence it's had into a movie."

Francine's eyes widened in shock.

"Great! I will have some documents emailed to you for you and your lawyers to review before we can continue."

"Okay, understood. Do you have my email?"

"Yes, my assistant has it. The email will come over shortly. I look forward to speaking to you soon."

"Thank you, Mr. Perry, we'll talk soon." Nelson hung up the phone then fist-pumped the air. "Yeah!"

Francine clapped excitedly.

***

Paul and Ronny were looking fly in their black Perry Ellis Slim-Fit Tuxedo. Each had a white calla lily in their lapel.

"You ready for this?" Paul asked Ronny standing by his side at the altar at the front of the church.

"I've been ready since the first day I laid eyes on Sofia." Ronny smiled. "Are you ready?"

"So ready this should've happened yesterday." Paul was marrying young at the age of twenty-one, almost twenty-two. But when you knew, you *knew*. And Lisa was it for him. He graduated early with his bachelor's degree in accounting. He works as a junior accountant at an accounting firm in Fort Washington, Maryland. He also has a side gig providing bookkeeping and accounting help to small businesses, he is fast on his way to working fulltime for himself within a year.

Ronny has a couple more years as an electrician apprentice before he can take the test to become a licensed electrician. He works as an electrician apprentice for a solar company in Beltsville, Maryland.

The large church that seats one thousand people was only filled with about one hundred close family and friends seated near the front. Everyone was dressed in their best dresses and suits for the occasion. The church was decorated with fresh white calla lilies and lace, simple yet elegant.

Thomas and Marcia had one of their one-year old twins in their lap. Marlana, sitting in her dad's lap, had on a cute pink frilly dress. Tiaan, sitting in his mom lap, wore a miniature suit. The twins were fed, well rested and full of giggles. Marcia and Thomas hoped they remained so throughout the ceremony. Jada, James and Karter with his date, were sitting in the front row with their parents and baby siblings.

The song "You" by Jesse Powell began to play. Paul and Ronny turned their attention to the double doors of the sanctuary that opened. The guests turned to face the doors as well.

Lisa was dressed in a mermaid style white wedding gown. Next to her Sofia wore a sweetheart neckline ball white gown. Their fathers stepped to their sides. Lisa and her biological father began walking down the aisle first, followed by Sofia and her father, the governor of Maryland. The couples chose a nontraditional wedding opting not to have bridesmaids and groomsmen. Ronny and Paul had tears in their eyes watching the love of their lives walk toward them. Twenty minutes later, Pastor Nelson pronounced the couples as husband and wife.

James graduated from high school and is attending college at Virginia Tech majoring in computer engineering. Jada is doing well as a junior in high school and recently received her driver's permit. Karter moved back to Maryland after he graduated college in California and is working as a Human Resources Specialist with the Department of State.

"You've got to be kidding me!" Marcia stood in the doorway of the twins' bedroom. One-year old Marlana and Tiaan were all smiles standing up in their cribs holding on to the railing. "Thomas!" Marcia shouted. `

Thomas walked out of their bedroom and met her in the kids' room. "Ewwww, who stinks?" He stopped in his track standing side by side with Marcia in the middle of the Noah's Ark themed room. Tiaan's diaper was off with poop smearing his butt, his crib sheet and crib railing. Tiaan stood giggling with his sister, whose diaper was still intact, in her crib across from his.

"Want to do rock paper scissors?" Thomas asked.

"Ugh! I always lose. Let's do heads or tails."

Thomas pulled his wallet from his jeans pocket and found a penny. "Heads or tails?"

"Head."

Thomas flipped the coin, caught it then placed it in his palm. Marcia leaned over to see. She reached up on her toes and kissed Thomas on the cheek. "I'll get Marlana, you take care of Mr. Poopie."

Thomas groaned. "We're not having any more kids." He moved toward Tiaan's crib.

"And you know this, man!" Marcia said in Chris Tucker's voice cracking herself up.

THE END

Awesome, you made it to the end.

Please leave a constructive review on Amazon/Goodreads or the site where book was purchased.

Thank you!

Also, check out other books by Khara Campbell.